## BEARS IN THE BARN

'James, don't you think we ought to fetch someone?' Mandy pictured them coming face to face with a frightened racoon, even a fierce bobcat.

Too late. The creature, or creatures, came padding along the boards. There was a sharp growl, heavy breaths, then a pair of small eyes staring down at them.

'Ida!' James grasped the ladder.

'And the cubs!' Mandy saw the two smaller faces peer over the edge of the loft, their broad noses twitching, their button-eyes bright. 'What are you doing up here?'

'Stealing apples from my fruit loft, that's what!' Dusty Owen stood framed in the open doorway, his legs wide apart, his shotgun raised and ready to fire.

LUCY DANIELS

# Bears

## — *in the* —

# Barn

*Illustrations by Jenny Gregory*

**Hodder**
*Children's*
*Books*

a division of Hodder Headline plc

Dan pb col
99- 07065- 2275

**Special thanks to Jenny Oldfield**
**Thanks also to C. J. Hall, B.Vet.Med., M.R.C.V.S., for reviewing**
**the veterinary information contained in this book.**

Text copyright © 1998 Ben M. Baglio
Created by Ben M. Baglio, London W12 7QY
Illustrations copyright © 1998 Jenny Gregory

First published in Great Britain in 1998
by Hodder Children's Books

A Catalogue record for this book is available from the British Library

ISBN 0 340 69953 1

Typeset by Avon Dataset Ltd, Bidford-on-Avon, Warks

Printed and bound in Great Britain by
Clays Ltd, St Ives plc

Hodder Children's Books
a division of Hodder Headline plc
338 Euston Road
London NW1 3BH

# One

'It's true what they say: you *can* have too much of a good thing!' Adam Hope groaned. He heaved his backpack on to his shoulders.

Mandy grinned. 'And too many French fries!' Since her mum and dad had arrived in America, it seemed they'd done nothing but eat, drink and laze in the sun.

'I've put on ten pounds!' Adam Hope declared.

'You'll soon walk it off,' Mandy's mum told him. 'If Mandy and James have anything to do with it, they'll have you trekking up mountains in no time.'

Emily Hope looked happy to be leaving their shiny, giant motor home in a carpark at the edge of the forest. She gazed up at the Arkansan hills, ready to begin.

'How did I get talked into this?' Mandy's dad reminded them that he'd come for a rest. 'You know: watching the sun set over a calm sea; palm trees; the gentle lapping of waves on a pure white beach . . .'

'We've been there, done that!' Mandy broke in. She hitched her own pack on to her back. They'd just spent two days driving up from sun-drenched Florida, through Mississippi and Tennessee.

'Not for long enough, if you ask me,' he grumbled. 'Three perfect days on Blue Bayous, my paradise island, then you lot whisk me off to see the rest of America!'

Mandy had spent the whole summer on the island with her grandparents and their friends, Bee and Jerry Logan. She'd loved every minute. But when her parents and her best friend James Hunter had flown to join her from their home in Welford, Yorkshire, they'd carried out their plan to head north into the wild Arkansan countryside. 'There's so much to explore!' she insisted. 'Really, Dad, you'll love seeing all the wildlife in these mountains!'

'Are we sure we've got everything?' Mrs Hope made one last check before they set off on foot.

She slung her camera over her shoulder, and double-checked the motor home doors to see that they were locked.

'Including the kitchen sink, by the feel of it.' Adam Hope staggered the first few steps up the track.

'Camping stove?' Emily asked.

'Yep.' James tapped his rucksack. 'In here.'

'Torch?'

'One each.' Mandy had packed them herself.

'Binoculars?'

'Round Dad's neck.'

'And the map.' James had marked the route in red, deep into Devil's Valley, sticking to the track that followed Bear Creek. He'd slipped the map into a plastic envelope and put it in the front pocket of his fleece jacket.

'How many miles do we have to walk today?' Mr Hope peered up the worn trail. There was an arch of green branches and a tangle of roots; he could hear the distant sound of running water from the creek.

'Only twelve,' James said cheerfully. 'Then we reach our first campsite, at a place called Little Springs.'

'Twelve miles!' Mandy's dad yelped. 'Listen, couldn't you take pity on me and leave me here? I could look after the motor home for you, spend the days reading and taking naps while you did your exploring. How does that sound?' He made his knees buckle, his legs sag.

Mandy tutted. 'Grandad paddled all the way round Blue Bayous when he was here, and he never grumbled once!'

'Now, there's a challenge!' Emily Hope winked, then laughed outright as her husband sagged and gasped. 'You poor thing!'

But Mandy refused to feel sorry for him. 'You can do it, Dad. And you'll enjoy it once we set off. We'll see all sorts of animals in the forest: squirrels, rabbits, deer, racoons, possum, bobcats . . . bears!' She thought the last one on the list would be too much even for her dad to resist.

'I don't think so,' James cut in. He'd already fished out the map to study it. 'You don't see many bears in Arkansas these days.'

She frowned. 'Why do they call it the Bear State then?'

'They don't, not any more.' James traced his finger along the trail, showing Mr Hope the distance they had to walk. 'That was in the olden days. I read about it.'

*Trust James*, Mandy thought. *He would have to stick to what he'd read in a book.*

One of Mandy's dreams was to come across a beautiful, furry black bear knee-deep in the rushing water of a crystal stream, or snuggled in the fork of a stout tree, taking his afternoon nap.

Mandy's mum glanced at her crestfallen face. 'Never mind, there's always a chance,' she consoled her as she stepped into the shade of the overhanging oak trees and swung into her stride. 'After all, it's definitely the right kind of country.'

'Wild,' Mandy agreed, falling into step beside her mum. 'Hardly any houses, plenty of trees. Bears like that.'

'Plenty of mountains,' her father grumbled. 'They like that too.' He and James trailed along behind.

'But they died out in the 1950s,' James insisted. He didn't believe in getting their hopes up. You had to be realistic. He tucked the map back into his pocket and caught up with Mandy. 'There'll be loads of racoons, though!'

'They're good,' she admitted. 'You should see their cute faces, James! They look as if they're wearing bandit masks!' And she was off on her favourite subject. Animals big and small, smooth and furry, fat and thin. At home at Animal Ark it was dogs, cats, guinea-pigs and rabbits. Here in

America it was racoons, buffalo, bobcats . . . and bears. They'd walked for twenty minutes deep into the forest, with Mandy talking nineteen to the dozen, when they came to the bank of a fast-running stream.

'This must be Bear Creek.' James dug into his pocket for the map.

'Of course there are no bears any more, like you said!' Mandy grinned at James, then turned to wait. 'Where's Dad?'

'Here he is.' Her mum pointed to a solitary figure toiling up the slope behind them.

Unhitching her rucksack, Mandy swung it to the ground. 'Come on, Dad. What kept you?'

Mr Hope was breathing heavily, stooping under the weight of his tent and sleeping-bag. But there was a twinkle in his eye. 'Guess!' he said.

'No, really, Dad. How come you were so far behind?' She could tell by the look on his face that he'd seen something exciting.

'You're not going to believe this!' He looked back over his shoulder. 'I'm not sure I do myself.' He tapped the binoculars which he wore round his neck. 'I double-checked through these to make sure.'

By this time, Mandy could hardly wait. 'What was it? A deer? A bobcat?'

He took a deep breath and shook his head. 'No. You know that clearing we just came through?' Mandy had been so busy talking about racoons to James that she'd hardly noticed.

'I got a good view of the mountain through the trees. And guess what? There was something moving quite high up. Just a dark speck. I couldn't tell what it was at first. Then I took another look. Of course, I still can't be absolutely sure . . .'

'Dad!' Mandy threatened to pounce on him and throttle him. 'What are you trying to say?'

'. . . Especially after what James was telling us about them being extinct in these parts. I got him in focus, then he went behind a rock and I had to wait until he came out again before I could see him clearly . . .'

'Dad!' Mandy did leap on him. He laughed and staggered backwards.

'He was down on all fours. At first I thought it could have been a small buffalo, but it was too furry for that; or a large deer, but it was too heavy. No, in the end there's only one thing it could have been.'

Mandy jumped in the air. 'A bear!' she cried. In the first half-hour after they'd left civilisation and begun to walk in the wild, her dad had spotted the very thing she'd dreamed about.

She left him standing and ran back to her mum and James. 'Dad's seen one!'

'One what?' James jumped up from the side of the creek.

'A bear!'

'Where?' asked James.

'On the mountain. It must still be up there. Quick, let's go and look!'

' "All Bears Are Dangerous!" ' James read the notice nailed on to the tree. ' "Keep A Clean Camp." '

Mandy carried on pitching her tent after the first day of the trek. The low sun cast long shadows through the tall pine trees. Little Springs campsite

was deep in Devil's Valley, miles from any road. 'What bears?' she grumbled.

She and James had spent the whole day searching, hoping to see the one that Adam Hope had spotted early that morning. They'd plunged through green oaks and maples tinged with gold. They'd followed old native American trails on to the bare mountains, then dipped back to the valley through swamps into silent green hollows. But they'd seen no sign of the bear.

'At least the notice proves they're here! I wonder why the books said they'd died out?' James was puzzled. He'd already pitched his own tent on a small gravel beach by the side of the stream. He'd taken off his baseball cap and flung it on top of his rucksack. Now he eased the laces of his walking-boots and peered at the board again. ' "Bears Enter This Campground. Use Extreme Caution."'

Mandy hammered tent pegs into the stony ground. 'We wish!' She longed for a bear to come ambling by. 'Dad, tell us again what he looked like!'

'Big and heavy. He kind of rolled as he moved along. Very hairy.' Adam Hope had taken off his boots and plunged his feet into the clear water. He sighed with pleasure.

'Sounds rather like you!' Emily Hope teased. She let her long red hair loose from its ponytail and sat down beside him.

'Uh-huh!' Mr Hope groaned, then grinned.

'How big?' Mandy wanted to know every tiny detail.

'About one-and-a-half metres tall on his hind legs, I guess. Difficult to tell from that distance.'

'What colour?'

'A kind of chocolate brown, with a white flash on his chest.'

'Sure it was a "he"?'

'Nope. Could have been female.' He wriggled his toes in the stream. 'See that mist,' he said to Emily. A low cloud had begun to form over the water, drifting into the hollows along the bank. The evening air was growing chilly after a baking hot day. 'On second thoughts, probably male,' he decided. 'On his own up there on the mountain, looking out for intruders. If it had been a female, she would've probably had a couple of cubs along with her at this time of year.'

Mandy nodded. Her tent was up; it was a bit wobblier than James's, but strong enough to shelter her for the night. 'So what *did* we see today?' she asked her friend when she saw him scribbling in his diary.

'Hang on, I'm making a list. Whitetail deer. How many?'

'Eleven.' The shy, delicate creatures had heard them crashing through the undergrowth looking for bears. They'd run off, their tails bobbing through the greenery. 'One dark grey bobcat with black spots, up that pine tree, remember?' They'd wondered at first what had made the scratch marks on the tough bark, then they'd looked up and seen the cat's yellow eyes staring down at them from the lowest branch.

James wrote swiftly. 'How many racoons?'

'Only four.' Racoons liked the early morning and evening for hunting, and spent the days hidden away from view. But the ones they'd seen had come in a small posse, rampaging through the woods, their little bandit-faces set straight ahead, and their ringed tails wafting behind them. Mandy let James go on with the list, and wandered off to a quiet rock which overlooked the misty stream. After a while, she heard her mum come to join her.

'Well?' Emily Hope sat down, drew her legs up to her chest and spoke quietly. 'Is it as good as you'd hoped?'

'Better.' Every minute, every second, brought something new: thin waterfalls streaming down a sheer cliff; springs bubbling up from under the worn limestone rock. There were woodpeckers tapping at the oak trees and blue herons resting one legged in the creek. Mandy had seen a wild turkey and heard him gobble. Her dad had stood by the water and pointed out trout, bass and bluegill.

'But?' her mum prompted. Her smile as she stared into the slow current was warm and relaxed.

Mandy sighed. 'How do you know there's a "but"?'

'With you, I just know!'

'OK then. *But* we didn't get to see the bear!' Mandy exclaimed.

'Not yet. Plenty of time.'

Time to unpack the stove and get out the pans. Time to cook supper in the glow of the gaslight that Adam Hope hung from a nearby branch. Then bed, which was an unrolled sleeping-bag inside a tiny canvas dome; and sleep to the sound of the screech-owl outside and strange, small scufflings in the bushes. But no heavy, padding feet, no big shadow, no bear grunts and snuffles.

Mandy lay awake for a long time, hoping. 'Tomorrow,' she breathed, hearing every twig snap, every leaf rustle. 'Or the day after.'

She fell asleep at last, convinced that the bears were out there. She pictured their hairy faces and round ears, and their brown, shiny, button-eyes.

# Two

For two more days they trekked through Devil's valley towards Omaha Springs. Bear Creek cut deep through limestone cliffs, then wound its way between sloping upland pastures dotted with white sheep. Lonely, wooden-built farmhouses with battered pick-ups parked in the yard and small boats moored by quiet jetties overlooked the clearings.

'Arkansas is so . . . empty!' James had started to count the number of people they saw each day. Today, Thursday, it was already five o'clock in the afternoon and he'd only counted three. 'One man fishing in the river back at Cherokee Point, a

farmer driving some sheep along a track, and one
lone hiker we saw at midday.'

The hiker had met them on the track. Dressed
in a faded blue T-shirt, jeans and light fawn boots,
he'd stridden towards them, and paused to say 'Hi'.

'Have you seen any bears?' Mandy had asked.

'Hundreds!' he laughed. 'No, seriously, you
might see one or two if you're lucky.' He dropped
his bag from his shoulder, ready to tell them about
bears in Arkansas. 'They're pretty rare. At one
time we were down to a couple of dozen in this
part of the state, and there were no bears at all in
the whole of Missouri and Oklahoma.'

'How come?' James wanted to know what had
happened.

'Hunters got 'em all. The bear's a useful sort of
animal. You can use his skin, his meat, his
grease . . .'

Mandy shuddered.

'On top of that, your average farmer is no friend
of the black bear. He'd as soon shoot one as shake
your hand.'

*Where had they heard that before*, Mandy wondered.
*In Australia, Africa and back home in England there
were similar struggles between farmers and native
wildlife.*

Their friendly young hiker read her disgusted

frown. 'You can't exactly blame them,' he explained. 'Bears are curious guys. They come poking around the farms, looking for food, never mind the crops they stamp on or the orchards they ruin. Anyhow, you'll be pleased to know not everyone agreed with the hunters and farmers. A few years back scientists like me came along and said it was a scandal that black bears were vanishing so fast from America's Bear State.'

'You're a scientist?' Mandy looked doubtfully at his T-shirt and wavy fair hair that flopped forward over his sunburned face.

'Sure. My name's John McCann. I've been up at Omaha Springs for the past month, carrying out a study programme on a particular bear we reintroduced a while back. He's an adult male, twelve years old, chocolate brown colour phase with white crest, home range of 40 square miles . . .'

'Chocolate brown?' Mandy interrupted. 'Dad saw one like that, didn't you, Dad?' She described the time and place. 'Would it be the same one?'

'Most likely. We named him Charlie Brown. A big, dark bear? There aren't too many like him around.'

John told them he'd finished his spell of study and was heading home to Little Rock, leaving a fellow scientist in the forest to carry on the work.

James listened eagerly. 'Is that how you stop the bears becoming extinct? You plan a programme to move them back into the area, then you study them to see how they get on?'

'You got it,' John told him. 'You like the sound of that kind of conservation work?'

'Yep.' James nodded eagerly.

Emily Hope told him he'd be good at it. 'It's a bit like being a detective, a cameraman, a journalist and a hunter all rolled into one. You need to think straight and follow tiny clues, then make proper records of what you see.'

James blushed.

'You would be really good!' Mandy agreed, as her dad said goodbye to John McCann and they prepared to carry on.

'You have a nice day now,' the young scientist had said. 'And good luck with spotting old Charlie Brown!'

They'd set off again with a new spring in their step. But that had been hours ago, and by teatime their hopes were beginning to fade.

'Never mind. There's always tomorrow,' Emily Hope said. She was studying the map, judging how far they had to go before they reached the ranch at Omaha Springs.

'And tomorrow, and tomorrow . . .' Adam Hope boomed in a deep voice. 'What do you say we camp here for the night?' He looked round at a gently sloping hillside that was clear of the tall pines and ancient oaks. The sun was still warm, and there was a flat area of land by the water's edge for their tents. A few hundred metres further on, the limestone cliffs rose steeply again, and the track grew hard.

'I reckon the ranch is just beyond this next stretch of cliffs, past that bend in the river.' Mrs Hope pointed on the map. They took a vote and agreed to stop. Soon the tents were up and tea was brewed.

Restless as ever, and disappointed not to have seen the great Charlie Brown, Mandy and James left the grown-ups to enjoy their hot drinks and wandered off towards the cliffs. Knee-deep in long, golden grass and red poppies, they felt the last heat of the day on their arms and faces.

'Hear that?' James said, stopping to listen. They were out of sight of the tents, around the bend in the river.

'No, what?'

'Nothing.' Only a lazy hum of insects and silence. 'Didn't you know you could hear nothing?' he teased. 'The sound of silence!'

'No, you can't!' Mandy was ready to argue. Not seeing the bear had made her scratchy. But then her ears did pick up something above the hum of insects and the ripple of water over smooth stones. 'OK, James, did you hear that?'

He wrinkled his nose. 'You can't fool me!'

'No, really, I did hear something. Listen!'

There it was again; a definite splashing in the water. This time, James nodded. His eyes lit up. 'It couldn't be . . . ?' he gasped.

'It could!' Mandy was already racing towards the next bend. Whatever was in the river was making plenty of noise.

'Could be a fisherman,' James warned, running after her. 'Or a herd of deer come down to drink.'

'I don't think so!' The splashing went on. It was as if things were falling into the water, rolling and splashing. More than one, definitely.

'It can't be Charlie Brown.' James came alongside. 'He'd be by himself!'

'What then?' For a few moments, the splashing stopped. Mandy and James pulled up and began to creep forward more quietly. 'Shh!' She put her finger to her lips. 'We don't want to scare them off.'

They reached the angle in the river, and crouched beneath a bulging part of the cliff where the water had eaten into its base. Down on all fours, half hidden by a bank of pebbles, they peered around the bend.

The first bear they saw had stumbled out of the water on to dry land. The sun was low behind him, and when he shook his shaggy, honey-brown coat, a million golden droplets scattered in every direction. Once more he shook, waggling his backside, his legs wide apart. The drops sprayed everywhere until the baby bear was dry.

'It's only a cub!' Mandy whispered. She gasped as the youngster pricked his round ears and stood on his hind legs to peer over the sea of fawn grass that reached up the slope beyond the cliff.

'And another!' James saw a second small bear charge out of the water and bundle himself against the first. They fell, locked in each other's arms, tumbling down the bank and into the water with a loud splash.

Two bedraggled baby bears came to the surface and swam. Noses above the water, ears laid flat, they paddled with all their might.

Then they were out of the water and scrambling across the pebbles, chasing, somersaulting and rolling into the stream. Noiseless, full of the joys of life, the bears continued their game.

Until the mother bear lumbered into sight. She

came downstream on all fours, her big paws smacking into the shallow water, kicking up a wake of white spray. Big and honey-brown like her cubs, her thick coat shone in the sunlight. Her black nose sniffed the air, and her ears were up. *Whack!* A front paw shot out as she reached the twins. She fetched one a box on the ears. *Stop fooling around! There's serious work to be done.*

At once they followed their mother out of the water on to a dry rock about a metre above water level, shaking themselves dry one last time.

'What are they doing?' Mandy breathed. She craned her neck to see.

'Staring at the water.' James watched the cubs stay close to their mother, good as gold, while she leaned forwards and peered into the swirling current. 'I think she's fishing!'

And sure enough, after the bear had stood motionless for less than a minute, out flashed one of the massive paws. The curved claws shone, she swiped the water, and hooked out a glistening trout. *Snap!* She caught it in her savage jaws. The fish struggled briefly, then was still.

'Supper!' Mandy breathed.

She sat back on the pebbles and sighed. At last! Not Charlie Brown the chocolate-coloured bear that they'd heard about, but the surprise of a

beautiful, golden-brown mother bear and her two cubs.

'Talk about skill!' James whispered. He watched the female come down from the rock on to dry land to divide the fish between the three of them. Then he turned to Mandy. 'So why didn't John McCann mention them?'

She was back beside him, watching the bears clean themselves up after their meal. Mother bear licked her babies with her long, pink tongue. The cubs wriggled and squirmed. 'Maybe he didn't know they were here,' Mandy suggested.

'That's not likely.' James frowned. 'Those scientists should know everything about the bears around here. And look, she seems to be in a hurry now.'

The bear was nosing the cubs up the bank, alert to the dangers of crossing an open field. She shepherded them speedily towards the cover of trees further up the slope.

Mandy stood upright to watch them go. 'Yes, you're right.' The mother bear was definitely nervous. 'Perhaps she caught our scent.' She felt sad that three creatures were rushing away. They were already at the fringe of the forest, disappearing into the shadows. But now Mandy could hardly wait to report back to her mum and dad.

'Are you coming?' she asked James.

He stood for a moment, his forehead still creased into a frown. 'It didn't feel like they were scared of *us*,' he insisted.

'You mean there was something else we couldn't see?' She thought of how the mother had put a stop to the cubs' noisy game as she came lumbering downstream, how she'd bustled them quickly up the hill.

'Or like they weren't meant to be here. Like they don't belong.' James thought it through. 'But it doesn't make sense, Mandy. What could a bear be scared of?' They were big and powerful enough to face any animal in the forest.

'Another bear?' She thought of Charlie Brown roaming the upper slopes, protecting his territory.

James jutted out his chin and spoke slowly. 'How about human beings?'

Hunters with traps and snares. Farmers with guns. Mandy, like James, knew that man was the only real enemy that the mother bear had to fear.

# *Three*

'James, Mandy – this is Mr Owen. He owns this sheep farm,' Emily Hope told them as they raced back to the tents with the news about the family of bears.

A tall man with long grey hair and a dark, bushy beard greeted them. 'Hi. Call me Dusty. Most everyone does.' When he smiled, his weather-beaten face creased into hundreds of tiny lines. On his head he wore a soft-brimmed hat with a camouflage pattern in brown and green, battered out of shape after years of wear.

Mandy and James stopped in their tracks. They knew it would be impolite to gabble out their news straight away.

'Dusty lives at Omaha Springs. He owns the land we're camping on,' Mr Hope explained. 'He came down from the ranch specially to see if there was anything we needed.'

'My wife, Marie, she sent down this here jar of honey.' The soft-spoken sheep farmer took the gift out of the pocket of his denim jacket and gave it to Mrs Hope. 'That's clover honey, collected right here in Omaha Springs.'

'Thank you, that's very kind.'

Mandy watched her mum put the jar on the small camping table that she'd set out for supper. There was bread and cheese, fresh fruit, and pasta boiling on the stove.

Meanwhile, Dusty Owen sniffed and cleared his throat. 'You won't mind me telling you, ma'am, it ain't good to set your food out in the open like that.'

Emily Hope looked concerned. 'For hygiene reasons?' Straight away she took the cheese and bread and wrapped them in foil.

'No, ma'am. I'm talking about bears.' The old farmer's eyes disappeared behind wrinkles of loose skin as he frowned and explained.

At the word, "bears" Mandy opened her own eyes wider. She almost butted in with her story of the bears fishing for their supper not two hundred metres from where they stood. But James jabbed her in the ribs with his elbow to stop her. Instead, she grimaced and listened.

'We've got a bear in these hills right now. And if he gets wind of something he likes the smell of, he'll be down here to steal your supper before you can turn around!'

Mrs Hope thanked Dusty for his advice. 'What else can I do to make sure he doesn't pay us an unwelcome visit?'

'You just keep all your food sealed nice and tight in one of those plastic boxes,' the farmer said slowly, pointing to the airtight containers that Mandy's mum carried in her rucksack. 'And another thing; don't bury your garbage when you leave. That old bear will smell it and dig it up before you know it. So take it with you. Otherwise you turn him into what we call a nuisance bear, meaning he'd keep on coming back the next day and the next day, looking for more food. If he doesn't get it, he could turn nasty.'

Mrs Hope promised to be careful and do as he asked. 'Is there only the one bear we have to look out for?'

The question set Dusty Owen off on a long, slow grumble. His gravelly voice rolled along with an easy southern drawl, but his lined face gathered seriousness as he talked. 'Ma'am, if you'd asked me that question a couple of days back, my answer would have been yes. Just the one old bear roaming up there, mostly minding his business, making sure no rival bear was fool enough to stray on to his patch. They like a whole lot of space, see.'

'So what happened to change things?' Adam Hope kept glancing at Mandy and James. He could read Mandy like a book; he knew that she was holding back some important information.

'I come down to breakfast yesterday morning, I look out of the window facing on to the apple orchard where Marie keeps her beehives, and I see them ripped to pieces, every last one of them.' Dusty shook his head. 'I know right away only a bear can do that. I guess it's the old brown bear, but soon see I'm wrong. There they are, right there in my orchard. Three of them: mom and two cubs. I ain't never seen them before. 'Course, Marie's real upset about her beehives.'

'What did you do?' Mr Hope looked sideways at Mandy and James, warning them to keep quiet.

'I went right out and yelled as loud as I could. I took my shotgun with me and waved it at them.'

Mandy frowned. Shotgun? How could he even think about shooting the defenceless cubs?

'I can't use the darned thing, of course. No permit to shoot a bear, see!'

Mandy sighed with relief.

'Plastic bullets or pepper spray! That's what the state governor says we can use to keep bears off our land.' The old man snorted. 'Pepper! Can you believe that?'

'Not much use, eh?' Adam Hope took his point.

'You ain't seen Marie's beehives,' Dusty Owen retorted. 'Wrecked. And all I can do is yell and spray pepper at the critters that did it. Now if you folks finish your supper here, and you care to come up to the house for coffee when you're done, I can show you just what I mean!'

'How come black bears can be pale brown?' Mandy asked James as they finished their meal, packed away every last crumb of leftover food and set off up the hill towards the ranch house, a little way behind Mandy's parents.

She was glad now that James had warned her to keep quiet about the three honey-brown bears in the creek. Although she felt sorry for the kind old rancher and his wife, she felt even more strongly that America's native bears should be given every chance. After all, there was plenty of room in this country for everyone.

'They come in colour phases,' James explained. When he was curious about something, he would read everything he could lay his hands on. 'You get black, chocolate brown, cinnamon, blond and honey. In one place, up in the north, you can even get a *white* black bear!' He grinned and fixed his glasses firmly on his nose.

'Did you see how quickly she caught that fish?' Mandy recalled the skill of the mother bear. 'She kind of scooped it and shoved it in her mouth in one go.'

'The toes on their front paws are like fingers,' James reported. 'It means they can even pick berries with them. And dig for roots. That's what they mostly eat – plants. Plus some insects and fish. And you know, they're incredibly clever.'

'No need to tell *me*.' Mandy looked ahead at the track that led steeply up the hill and through a thicket of young oak and hickory to the ranch house beyond. Further still she could see a huge mountain range. The hills nearby started off green. In the distance they shaded off to deep blue, then hazy grey. The air above was clear and thin.

'. . . Long memories,' James went on. 'They can remember where to find food from years before and go back to the exact same spot! Did you know, a single black bear can eat twenty-five thousand caterpillars in one day!'

'You'd think the farmers would like them then,' Mandy argued. 'If only they could see their uses as well as their drawbacks.'

'And three thousand hazelnuts!'

Not so good. Nuts could be seen as crops, like honey. 'Who's counting?' she muttered, wondering how James managed to remember these weird and wonderful statistics.

'Scientists like John McCann, I expect.' Giving up on Mandy, James ran ahead to join Adam Hope, who would no doubt share his enthusiasm for bear facts and figures.

The Owens' ranch house had just come into view; it was a white, two-storey wooden building with green shutters and a porch along the front. It stood in a clearing, with lawns at the front and sloping rows of apple trees behind. Then came a white fence, and beyond that the green slopes where Dusty Owen farmed his sheep.

'Remember, we're guests here.' Mandy's mum had caught her up from behind. 'I know what you're probably thinking, "Equal Rights for Bears!" and all that.'

'I never said a word!' Mandy thought she'd been super-polite to Mr Owen.

'You don't have to,' her mum grinned. 'Your face is like an open book! I saw how you looked when he mentioned having a shotgun. Your eyes were blazing!'

'Well, honestly!' It was time to tell her mum what she and James had seen in the creek. 'It must have been the same three bears,' she insisted. 'No wonder the poor things looked nervous, if they've had people pointing guns at them!'

'Nevertheless, I don't want you to be rude to the Owens,' Mrs Hope insisted. 'Just watch and listen. There's an awful lot to learn about life here if you keep your eyes and ears open. We might not agree with everyone all of the time, but understanding other points of view is important.'

Mandy sighed, then agreed. 'But we don't have to tell Mr Owen that we spotted the bears, do we?' She didn't think she could go so far as to do that.

Emily Hope shook her head. 'No need. From what he told us, it sounds like they're a bit like us; just passing through. They'll probably be gone by tomorrow.'

Reassured, Mandy strode on to catch up with James and her dad as they came to the fence.

'What I wouldn't give right now for a nice, hot cup of coffee!' Adam Hope linked arms with

Mandy, opened the white gate and marched up the sloping lawn to the house.

'It's so great to relax!' Mandy's dad sat with his feet up on the Owens' porch. He took his time, sipping the drink and listening to Dusty's fisherman stories about the giant fish in the creek that had got away.

Marie Owen sat smiling in the doorway. She was a stout little lady with grey hair pinned back in a bun, bright, dark eyes and three chins that wobbled when she laughed. The buttons of her cardigan strained to stay fastened across her chest, and she wore a faded flowered apron with a torn pocket and frayed edges. Mandy liked her from the start.

'To hear Dusty talk, you'd think the fish in that creek lived just to jump on to his hook and then jump right off again!' She laughed now, running the flat of her work-worn hand back from her forehead over her smooth hair. Then she turned to Emily Hope. 'What about Adam? Does he go fishing?'

'He doesn't have time.' Mandy's mum told the Owens about their life back home. 'We run a vet's practice called Animal Ark in Yorkshire so we're always busy.'

'You're a veterinarian?' Marie Owen seemed surprised. She looked thoughtful as Mrs Hope described their work.

'We're a country practice, but these days we work mostly with small animals. A lot of domestic pets – cats, dogs, rabbits, guinea-pigs and so on. Sometimes we get called out to the farms, but perhaps not so often as in the old days.'

'Farms, huh?' The old lady's bright eyes narrowed.

'Sheep, cows, horses. There's still quite a lot of vaccination work, and we go out to assist at difficult births if a farmer gives us a ring.' Emily Hope was too modest to tell her that the Hopes at Animal Ark were known as the best vets in the dale.

'Sheep, huh?'

'Yes. As a matter of fact, the farms in Yorkshire aren't so different from here. It's the same sort of country: limestone and sandstone, plenty of streams and waterfalls. And it's pretty hilly, so a lot of the land isn't cultivated. Where the moors meet the pastures, it's given over to sheep farming.'

'Like here?' Marie Owen seemed set on repeating Emily's ideas.

'Except for the temperature,' Adam Hope put

in. 'We could do with heat like this in Welford!'
He stretched his arms behind his head and leaned
back still further.

'Well now, I have a couple of sheep here in the
barn that need some attention,' Marie confessed
at last. 'It's been on my mind to bring the veterinarian up from Lost Valley, but it's quite a drive . . .'

'No need.' Emily Hope got to her feet. 'Now
that we're here, why don't I take a look instead?'
She didn't hesitate to offer her help.

'But you're on vacation,' Dusty cut in.

'I don't mind at all.' She was quite definite.
'Mandy, do you want to come and take a look?'

Mandy, too, was quick to say yes.

'I see you're following in your mom and dad's
footsteps,' Marie Owen said, as she led them slowly
around the back of the house. 'I'm not getting
any younger,' she sighed, pausing for breath under
the apple trees. The bark on some nearby trees
was torn and scratched. 'Darned bears,' she
muttered, noticing Mandy examining the marks.
'That's where they dug their claws in to climb up
and get at my apples.'

Mandy pictured the mother bear shinning up
the smooth bark, clutching the trunk until she
reached the fruit. Maybe the cubs would follow.
Looking up into the branches, she saw that there

were hardly any apples left on the tree.

'I guess you think they're sweet, cuddly things.' Marie led them on towards a big wooden barn with a high roof. 'Teddy bears with soft fur and cute faces.'

'Oh no, I don't think of them like that.' Mandy wanted her to know that she was more realistic.

But Marie went on regardless. 'Believe me, there's nothing cuddly about an American black bear. See over there? That's what left of my beehives!'

They looked to where she was pointing, beyond the orchard, to a row of wooden hives. All were damaged. Rooves had been torn off, and whole hives destroyed.

'Best clover honey,' Marie grumbled, turning away with a shrug. 'All gone. No, there's nothing cute about 'em!'

Mandy remembered her mum's instructions and kept quiet. She understood what the bears' raid must mean to the Owens; lots of work to repair the hives, and no money from selling the honey to the local shops and markets. Not to mention the apples the bears had scrumped. Quietly, she followed Mrs Owen and her mum into the warm, sweet-smelling barn.

'Take these, for instance!' The rancher's wife

opened the door of a stall and showed them two young sheep, little more than lambs. They lay on a bed of straw, looking up and bleating feebly. 'They look OK now, but you should have seen 'em when Dusty brought 'em in. Blood everywhere.'

While Mandy looked over the side of the stall, Emily Hope crouched down to see what was wrong.

'Merinos.' Her mum correctly identified the breed from their white faces and legs and their thick, woolly coats. She pointed out their injuries to Mandy. 'See this nearest one? There's a gash on its front leg, and its ear has been torn. The other one has a cut along its cheek.'

Mandy nodded. 'What happened?' she asked Marie Owen.

'Dusty brought 'em down from Wolf Point early yesterday. It's the highest mountain round here, a pretty cut-off sort of place, well out of sight of the house. Says he found 'em lying by a rock. They were in a bad way. We didn't know if we could save 'em.'

'You did a pretty good job.' Emily Hope examined the wounds. 'Nice and clean. No infection.' The sheep lay quietly as she turned its head and ran her fingers up and down the injured leg.

Mrs Owen grunted. 'No bones broken?'

'Not as far as I can tell. No, as long as the wounds stay clean, I don't think you've any reason to worry too much. Give them plenty to drink, keep them quiet. It'll take a couple of days for them to get over the shock.' She stood up and backed out of the stall. 'I have some antibiotics in my bag back at camp. Mandy, will you run and fetch them for me?'

'No, really . . .' The old lady was embarrassed. 'You've done enough by setting my mind at rest. Thank you.'

'It's no trouble.' Mandy was eager to help. She peered in again at the sturdy young sheep, still wondering what had happened. 'Was it an accident? A fall of some sort?' Maybe they'd got caught in razor-wire, or stumbled down a hidden gulley.

But Marie Owen shook her head, and Mandy turned to the barn door. Dusty stood there, casting a long shadow across the bales of straw stacked behind the stall. 'That's no accident!' he protested.

'Go on, Mandy, fetch me those antibiotics!' Emily Hope reminded her. She gave her a little push out of the door.

'Accident!' Mr Owen stood in the way. 'No, that's bears for you!'

Mandy stared at him. 'They attacked the sheep?

Are you sure?' She forgot her mum's instructions, forgot all her earlier advice. 'Bears don't normally attack sheep, do they? Did you see it happen? Couldn't it have been something else?'

'Oh, sure!' Dusty didn't like being challenged. 'I've only lived here for seventy years. What would *I* know?'

'But – did you actually – see?' Mandy stammered. Her mum was frowning at her. James and her dad were striding across the farmyard to join them.

'It's gotta be bears!' The old farmer turned and appealed to Adam Hope as he took him into the barn to investigate. 'You see these injuries? A bear's claws, that's what did that!'

'You mean, after the apples and the beehives, they went up on to the pastures and attacked the sheep?' Mr Hope considered it quietly.

'Sure!' By now, Dusty had worked himself up. He took out his irritation on Mandy, determined to give her a lesson in bear habits, making it clear she didn't know the first thing about sheep farming in the shadow of Wolf Point.

As she backed off into the yard, Dusty Owen stabbed his finger towards her. 'One time, when I was young, we just about got rid of bears from the entire state, and I was a happy man, I can tell you that!'

'Now, Dusty.' His wife stepped forward. 'Don't go so hard on the girl.'

'She should know this,' he insisted. 'Now the bears are back, and it's all the fault of some fool scientists! They want to "bring back the bear to his native land"!' Dusty mimicked the high-minded tone of those who were on the side of the bears. 'And me? I can't shoot 'em, I can't raise a finger to stop 'em destroying my crops and killing my critters!'

'Now it's not her fault,' Marie tried to remind him. But her husband towered over Mandy and he hadn't finished.

'So whose fault is it?' he demanded, as Mandy backed off, her knees trembling, her mouth dry. Then turning towards his wife, Dusty continued. 'You ask her whose side she's on, and she'll tell you she wants the bears back in these mountains. They always do. That's why the scientists get to go ahead with the stupid scheme. Now me? Put a shotgun in my hands and show me a bear. He'll soon find out if I want him on my land. Yes sir, you bet!'

# Four

'How *can* Dad go fishing with Mr Owen?' Mandy wondered. It was early next morning, and she was pulling on her boots with impatient tugs. The laces were too tight, and she couldn't slide her foot inside.

'Very easily.' Emily Hope took Mandy's bad mood in her stride. 'You have to remember that Dusty Owen is a decent, kind sort of man.'

'Even after what he said?' She remembered how he'd yelled at her about the bears, raising an imaginary shotgun and pretending to get the bears in his sight.

Her mum nodded. 'Think of some of the

farmers back home and how they are about rabbits. You wouldn't hate Ken Hudson just because he takes a pot-shot to scare them off.'

'Ken's different.' He worked on the pig farm near Welford, and knew everything there was to know about farm animals. 'He cares!'

'How do you know Dusty doesn't care?' Mrs Hope slung her sleeping-bag over a tree branch and brushed out the floor of her tent. She wore her hair twisted on top of her head, and was already dressed in a long green sweatshirt and shorts. 'Think about it. He was probably worried about his sheep when he said what he did.'

'But, Mum, you didn't see the little bear cubs. We did.' Finally she had her boots on. Mandy stood up and stamped her feet, looking round for James. 'If you'd seen them, you couldn't possibly talk about shooting them!'

'I saw the beehives and the injured sheep,' Mrs Hope reminded her. 'And when Dusty realised he'd scared you over the bears, he did apologise. Anyway, your dad accepted his invitation, so it's something you'll have to live with.'

Adam Hope had set off in the misty dawn, heading for the creek, where he was to meet the old farmer for a morning's fishing. Mandy had seen a dreamy expression come over her father's face when Mr Owen had described his flat-bottomed rowing-boat, the clear water carrying them downstream, hours spent drifting with the current, or sitting on the bank waiting for the fish to bite.

'And meanwhile, I'm going to spend some time up at the ranch with Marie. I want to check on the injured sheep, then stay and have coffee. What do you and James plan to do?'

'Track the bears.' James poked his head out of his tent. He crawled out and spread the map on the ground to show Emily Hope the area he'd marked. 'We're going to look in this triangle here, starting at Bear Creek where we saw them yesterday, up to the ranch, where we know they've already been, and across to Wolf Point, where they attacked the sheep—'

'Maybe. Maybe not.' Mandy still had her doubts. 'But we reckon that if we cover that area, we stand a pretty good chance of seeing them again.' Just thinking about it gave her a warm, eager glow.

Her mum nodded. 'Unless they've moved on already.' She zipped up her tent, ready to leave. 'But if they have stuck around and you do come across them, remember not to go too close.' She laid down some safety rules. 'Use the binoculars and look from a distance. Make plenty of noise to warn them you're around. Don't take them by surprise.'

James listened carefully. 'It's OK, Mrs Hope, we'll be careful.'

'And be back here by lunchtime,' was her parting shot. 'I'll see you then.'

So they went their different ways, Mrs Hope up the hill on her visit to the old rancher's wife, James and Mandy down to the bend in the river where they'd first spotted the three bears.

By the time they arrived on the gravel beach, the mist had begun to lift, along with Mandy's spirits, and she'd managed to convince herself that the bears would be back in the same spot as before. They'd be round the bend in the river, play-fighting in the shallow stream. The mother would be stretched out along a low branch overhanging the water, one eye open and watching the cubs, the other closed and catching forty winks.

She and James crept together around the cliff, hearing the water rush over the boulders on the bank, and peered over the pebble bank.

'Oh!' Mandy's face fell. 'Hi, Dad. Hi, Mr Owen.'

No cubs playing, no mother bear snoozing, just the two fishermen lazing about in a boat.

'Hi, Mandy. What are you up to; not bear tracking by any chance?' Mr Hope grinned.

She stood up and scuffed the pebbles with her toe. 'Not really.' She didn't want to talk about bears with Mr Owen sitting in the boat, staring at them from under the brim of his battered hat.

'Have you caught anything?' James came out from under the cliff, anxious to change the subject.

'Not yet. But you should see the size of these trout!' Adam Hope held his hands wide. 'They're *this* big!'

'Yes, sir!' Dusty Owen leaned sideways to look down into the water. 'They sure are one heck of a size!'

Mandy and James left them to it and made a quick getaway. 'See you later!' Mandy called back as she sprinted up the bank through the long, golden grass.

'Hope you catch something!' James added, following close on her heels. 'Listen, Mandy, the best thing is to head straight up to Wolf Point. We're not going to find the bears where there are people around. If they're still here, they'll have found a nice quiet spot to sleep the day away.'

She agreed and they cut off across the hillside, heading to the woods behind the house. 'Maybe it's somewhere up here that Charlie Brown lives as well!' If they were lucky they might see all of the bears. It was high in the mountains that her dad had first spotted a bear through the binoculars.

Jogging steadily, they entered the shadow of the woods, where tall pine trees cut out most of the light. Here, the earth smelled damp and sharp, with the strong scent of pine needles crushed underfoot. Rocky outcrops pushed through the earth, and the slope grew steeper. Soon their jog became a walk and then a slow scramble through ferns, across trickling streams and out of the woods on to bare rock.

'Hang on!' James stopped to pull out the map. He drew a deep breath as he studied where they were. 'That's Wolf Point over there; the one with the highest rocks!' He pointed to a bare, steep hillside dotted with sheep. 'Maybe we should begin to look properly now.'

Mandy agreed. She used the binoculars to scan the hills. Once she got them into focus, she found she could see every rock and bush, even the rough surface of the bark on the isolated trees that managed to grow in the shadow of Wolf Point. 'Bobcat,' she said softly, handing the binoculars to James. 'By the dead pine tree.' She'd seen the grey, spotted cat slink out from behind a rock, and recognised its short, stumpy tail, and its large, tufted ears.

'It's big!' James breathed. 'About twice the size of a normal cat!'

'I bet it could attack sheep, especially young ones,' Mandy said thoughtfully. She turned to look at James.

He nodded. 'It looks strong enough.' Scanning away from the wild cat, he stopped on another moving speck in the distance. 'Take a look at this!'

Mandy took the binoculars and found the spot on a hilltop way beyond Wolf Point. It was almost too far away to make out, but the more she looked, the more sure she grew. 'Do you think it could be Charlie Brown?' she said softly.

'No need to whisper. He can't hear you,' a stranger's voice interrupted.

Mandy and James swung around to see a smallish man laden with cameras, binoculars and plastic wallets, which he wore strung round his neck. His worn jeans and faded denim jacket, together with his round-rimmed glasses, gave him a studentish air. He'd crept up on them without a sound.

'Good work!' he told them. 'You just spotted our very own *Ursus americanus*!' Coming to introduce himself, he grinned at their surprise. 'American black bear. Otherwise known as Charlie Brown! Hi, I'm Frank Crews. You must be from the group

John McCann met when he was heading off home to Little Rock!'

'How did you know?' James had handed the binoculars back to Mandy and was still staring at the newcomer.

'We're part of the same team. He rang me last night at camp, told me all about you. Said you seemed pretty keen to see Charlie. Well, now you've seen him!'

'Yes, but . . .' Mandy was scouring the far hillside again.

'But not close enough, huh?' The young scientist picked up her meaning. 'Can't get to feed him and take pictures? Yeah, Charlie's kind of shy.'

'I can't see him. He's gone.' She sighed as she lowered the binoculars.

'So, what do you want to know?' Frank Crews seemed to be in no hurry. He reeled off a few facts. 'Charlie's nearly two metres long, he weighs 300 kilos. Herbivore. Eats hardly any meat. Large head, small ears, massive shoulders. Plantigrade posture—'

'Hold on!' James had come across a fact he didn't know. 'Planti – what?'

'It means he walks on the whole surface of his foot, heels down. Not like a cat, see?' Frank mimicked the walk. 'Not built for speed, but he's made strong instead. He has good limb mobility—'

'What?' This time it was Mandy's turn to be drawn in.

'Lots of movement in his joints. Makes him agile for his size. He can climb trees. He swims pretty well too.' The scientist paused for them to ask questions, then he had a better idea. 'Say, why don't I show you a couple of bear clues? You're in luck. I just found fresh droppings!'

'How fresh?' James wrinkled his nose.

Frank laughed. 'Too fresh to have been left by Charlie. No, I reckon they belong to this honey phase mother we have here right now.' He led off down the hillside, back towards the woods.

Mandy caught up with him. 'You know about her?'

'Sure. There's quite a story.' He showed them the place with the tell-tale droppings, then expertly scooped some into a plastic bag. 'When I send these to the lab, they'll tell us what she's had to eat these last twenty-four hours.'

James held back, looking as if he was trying not to breathe. It made Frank laugh out loud. 'Say, this could be the closest you get to Ida! The droppings contain vital information about the bears we return to the wild.'

'Ida?' Mandy repeated the name, tingling with

excitement. 'We got closer to them yesterday, when they were fishing for supper.' She told him about the two cubs playing in the river.

'That would be Jack and Jill, like in the nursery song. They went up the hill.'

She nodded. He might be a scientist, but by the look in his eye Mandy could tell that Frank was as bear-mad as she was.

'Fifteen weeks old, one male, one female. John saw them while he was on duty here in the valley. He's the one who gave them their names.'

'How long have they been here? Does Charlie know about them? Doesn't he mind them being on his territory?'

'Slow down! Here comes the interesting part.' Frank put the specimen into his rucksack, then leaned against a nearby log pile. 'Ida came to Omaha Springs two days back. Sure, Charlie knew about if from the start. You could say he wasn't real pleased. If he got half a chance he'd attack the cubs, especially Jack. Male rival,' he explained, noting Mandy's shocked expression.

'Would he kill him?' James asked.

'Sure. So Ida has her work cut out keeping the cubs out of his way. She stands guard most of the day and most of the night. She'd fight back if Charlie tried anything, but he's a tough guy and he's twice her size!' Frank shrugged and picked up his bag. 'The sooner she takes the cubs out of here, the better.'

'But why did she come in the first place?' This was the part of the story Mandy didn't understand. 'Didn't she know about Charlie?'

'She didn't have any choice. Listen, Ida didn't *want* to bring her cubs here. Someone brought them in a truck and dumped them.' Frank's voice changed. He walked steadily thought the trees, down towards the ranch.

'How do you mean, "dumped"?' James was the first to collect his thoughts. 'How do you know?'

'It's like this. When John first came across these bears he knew they must be way off their home range, so he rang around. Did anyone know anything about a mother bear that had gone missing with her two cubs? It wasn't too hard to find out, 'specially since they were honey phase. That's pretty rare. So the answer comes back next day; yes, the bears were from an area just west of Little Rock, from a mountain range called Ida Falls, a hundred and thirty miles from here.'

'That's why he called her Ida,' James realised.

'Yep. And the babies are Jack and Jill, because he first saw them fooling around, falling down the hill at the back of the ranch, picking

themselves up and running right back up to start
again.'

Mandy smiled, then her face clouded over. 'But
why would anyone want to bring the bears all the
way from Little Rock and dump them here?'

'Farmers,' Frank said with another shrug. He
stopped within sight of Omaha Springs ranch
house. 'You know.'

'They don't like bears on their land!' James
cried. 'But can they just do that – catch bears and
truck them out?'

'Nope. It's against the law. It wrecks the state's
reintroduction programme. But that doesn't stop
them.' For the first time since they'd met him,
Frank wasn't keen to talk.

Mandy gathered her thoughts. 'So, OK, John
found out where Ida and her cubs were from. What
happens now?'

Immediately Frank cheered up. 'Here's the good
news. My bosses in Little Rock locate the bears'
home range on Ida Falls. They tell me to come
up here and forget about Charlie Brown for a week
or so. I have to switch the study to Ida.'

'Why is that good?' James pursued him with
another question as he skirted around the white
ranch fence and plunged down the slope towards
the river.

'Because it's something new.' Frank listed the reasons. 'Because this is a mother and her young cubs we're working with. And most of all, it's good because it gives me the chance to study the bear's fantastic homing instinct.'

'Meaning what?' It was Mandy's turn now. She tuned in to the scientist's excitement.

'Meaning that Ida, like all black bears, has a most incredible instinct for finding her way back to her home range. Put a river, a whole bunch of roads, even a mountain in her way and it makes no difference. That bear keeps on heading back. And now it's my job to track her as she goes.'

# Five

'But you told us it's a hundred and thirty miles to Little Rock!' Mandy stood on the spot, watching Frank Crews pause by a moss-covered tree.

'Yes, and you said the farmers brought Ida and the cubs here in a truck!' James added.

'Sure.' Frank jotted something in his notebook, then strode on through the meadow, knee-deep in red poppies. Below him, at the bottom of the slope, Bear Creek rippled and splashed along its lively course. 'Like I said, these bears find their way by pure instinct. It's a kind of mental map that takes them home, wherever they happen to be dumped.'

'Wow!' Mandy caught up with him. 'How's it work?' She had to wait for an answer; Frank was busy examining paw prints in the mud bank at the side of the creek.

'We don't know exactly how they do it. That's what makes it a great study. It's my job to follow their every move, never getting too close, making sure not to mess up their natural behaviour. Wherever they go, I go. When they stop, I stop. I write everything down and take pictures. In the end, I get a complete record of their trek back home!' He looked up and caught the gleam in Mandy's eye. 'Fantastic, huh?'

'Hang on.' James had thought of another question. 'Don't those farmers know about this homing instinct that bears have?'

'I guess.' Frank found more prints that interested him. 'But I reckon they figured a hundred and thirty miles was far enough. They may be right; one-thirty, one-fifty miles is about the limit. After that, you can dump a bear in a strange place and it won't have the first clue about how to get home.'

James nodded. 'So if Ida makes it, she'll be doing pretty well?'

'Especially with her cubs along with her.' Mandy realised the mother bear was up against a huge task. She envied Frank the job of tracking her.

'What if you lose her trail?' she asked.

'Don't even think about it!' Frank looked up and down the length of the stream. He admitted his job was difficult. 'Most times we have a radio tag attached to the bears. We give them a collar as soon as we trap them, before we put them on to their new home range. The collar sends out a signal which we pick up on a receiver. It lets us know exactly where they get to.'

'Has Charlie Brown got one?' James asked.

'Sure. He's part of our planned programme. But not Ida. So no radio tag, no signal.' Frank concentrated on a patch of bushes on the opposite bank. He listened hard. 'Hear that? Sounds like a boat, just around the bend there.'

'It's probably Mr Owen and my dad.' Mandy told him about the fishing trip. Looking at her watch, she saw it was almost lunchtime. 'They'll probably finish about now.'

'They could be in for a surprise,' Frank warned. He pointed to the bushes, and there was Ida, standing quietly watching the current. She was half-hidden by the thick green leaves, her head craning forward and her ears laid back. There was no sign of the cubs.

Mandy took a look through the binoculars. The bear's coat was shaggy and wet, and her sides

heaved as she caught her breath. 'Looks like she's already been in the water,' she whispered, handing the binoculars to James.

'There she goes!' Frank said, as Adam Hope appeared, rowing the boat all by himself. Ida seized her moment and launched herself from the bank. She landed with a splash that rocked the boat and sent Mandy's dad paddling frantically for the opposite shore. Mandy, James and Frank ran closer to the bank.

'Help!' He saw Mandy and the others standing there. Ida's clumsy dive had brought her to the surface and she was swimming strongly after the rowing-boat.

'Don't panic, Dad!' Easier said than done, Mandy knew. It must be terrifying to have nearly a hundred kilos of bear diving on top of you.

'Don't just stand there!' he yelled back. 'What do I do?' Ida was gaining on him, her huge head almost butting the back of the boat. Mr Hope paddled for all he was worth.

'OK!' Frank took over, wading knee-deep into the stream to shout instructions. 'Have you got any fish in the boat?'

'Three trout!' Adam Hope swung his oar behind him, swiping at Ida but missing. She lunged at the boat.

'Throw them out!'

'What?' Water splashed into the boat as he rocked from side to side.

'Throw them to the bear. It's what she's after!'

Mandy watched her dad lunge forward and pick up the slippery catch. He flung the fish one by one over the side, then kept on paddling. 'Dusty's gonna kill me!' he yelled.

'I am?' The old man had come scrambling down the bank to join them, just in time to see the morning's work go to waste. He saw Ida veer away from the boat to scoop the dead fish out of the water into her jaws; one, two, three. 'I sure am!' he moaned. 'What did you go and do that for?'

But Mandy and James kept their eyes glued on Ida, who swam with the fish wedged in her mouth back to the far bank. She heaved herself out of the water, and shook herself dry. She dropped the catch on the grass and gave a rumbling growl. The cubs came running out of the bushes.

'Lunch!' James said, grinning at Mandy.

'*My* lunch!' Dusty Owen didn't see the funny side. As Adam Hope landed the boat nearby, Dusty went to help him on to dry land. 'Are you gonna explain to Marie, or am I? I've already told her to light the stove and stand by.'

'Sorry.' Mandy's dad staggered up the bank. 'I

just did as I was told. Thanks.' He shook hands with Frank as James made the introductions. 'I was in a bit of trouble back there!'

'Ida wouldn't really have hurt you,' Mandy tried to tell him. He was soaked through. His shirt stuck to him, and his beard was dripping.

'Oh yeah?' Dusty pushed into the middle of the group. He'd realised who Frank was from James's introductions. 'You one of those fool scientists?' he demanded.

Frank frowned. Even at full height, he only came up to the tall rancher's shoulder. 'I belong to the state scheme to reintroduce bears into these hills,' he agreed. 'I don't know about being a "fool scientist".'

'State scheme!' Dusty grew speechless with anger. Not only had he lost his lunch, but it was due to the people he hated most, the ones responsible for the nuisance bears on his land. 'I turn my back for fifteen minutes and when I get back, there's a darned bear attacking this poor guy here who hardly knows what hit him . . . !'

'That's OK, really.' Adam Hope had got over his fright. He didn't want an angry scene.

'I'm sorry it turned out like this.' Frank, too, tried to calm Dusty down. 'But that bear you see over there doesn't belong to our scheme. As a matter of fact, she should only hang around for a couple of days, then she'll be gone.'

'Yeah, yeah!' Mr Owen tossed his head in the direction of the bears. Ida had shared the fish and was waiting for the cubs to finish eating. 'You asked her, did you? She gave you a written guarantee?'

There was no point trying to reason with him, as he turned and stormed up the hill.

'What do I know?' he yelled back. 'I only farmed this land for fifty years. You guys, on the other hand, know it all. You got college notebooks full of stuff! Yeah, you got all the answers!'

Mr Owen was gone, out of sight, striding back towards the ranch minus his lunch, with a great big chip on his shoulder.

'Phew!' Frank Crews breathed again. 'What did I say?'

'It's not your fault.' Adam Hope got James to check that the boat was safely moored, then offered the scientist a cup of coffee back at camp. 'Right now Dusty's ready to blame anyone who comes within shouting distance.'

Mandy was still watching the bears. The cubs had lost interest in the fish and gone tree climbing instead. Ida ate the scraps and ambled after them. 'Why, what happened?' she asked absent-mindedly.

Her father's answer brought her round with a

jolt. 'Dusty got called back to the farm about an hour ago,' he explained. 'Marie came and fetched him. He left me with the boat.'

'What was so important?' James asked.

'That's just it. It's the reason he's in such a bad mood again,' Adam Hope told them. 'Marie came to tell him that another sheep's been badly mauled. He had to go and see if he could help Emily to save it!'

'How did you get on?' James ran to meet Emily Hope as she made her way back to the camp. It was early afternoon, and they'd had no further word about the emergency at the ranch. 'How's the injured sheep?'

Mandy couldn't bear to listen. There was something in the way her mum walked, head down, hands in pockets, that told her the answer before she spoke.

Mrs Hope came and sat down on the grass. 'No good. We did our best, but . . .'

Adam Hope gave her a sympathetic smile.

'The problem was it had lost too much blood. We think the attack happened much earlier this morning, but Marie and I only came across it just before lunch, when we were out taking a stroll.' She spoke quietly, taking the cup of coffee that

Mandy handed to her. 'Thanks, love. It was another young one. It seems that whatever is doing this leaves the fully-grown sheep alone. Similar injuries as to the other two – deep cuts around the face. This one had the worst injury at the base of its skull, as if the attacker came up from behind.'

'And does Mr Owen think that it's Ida?' James wanted to know. He explained to Mandy's mum all they'd learned from Frank about the honey-coloured bear and her cubs.

'He seems one hundred per cent sure that it is. You can't really blame him; every time one of his sheep is attacked, the bear is sighted nearby. Poor man, he stands to lose money if this goes on!'

Mandy listened glumly, glad when Frank Crews broke in. 'Hi, Mrs Hope. What was your guess? Did it look like the work of a bear?'

She shook her head. 'I couldn't be sure. I'd have said the wounds looked more like teeth marks than claws. Of course, it's hard to say.'

'Sure. But I'd question Mr Owen's opinion too, as a matter of fact.' The young man spoke earnestly, his feelings breaking through the dry reasons he put forward. 'For instance, food is plentiful for the bears right now. More berries than they can eat, and plenty of fish. Why would Ida attack the sheep? It's not her normal first choice of food source. And if she did want the meat, why didn't she finish these sheep off? She's strong enough to kill them with one swipe of her paw.'

'I know.' Mrs Hope agreed. 'But it wasn't the time to tell Dusty and Marie they might be wrong. They're upset and worried. I said I'd call back and see how they were later this evening.'

Everyone agreed that it was better to leave it for now. Besides, Mandy and James were keen to spend the afternoon with Frank. 'We could help you make notes and take photographs – if that's OK with you!' Mandy remembered her manners just in time.

Frank grinned and checked with Mr and Mrs Hope. 'Sure. But after lunch is snooze time for bears,' he reminded them. 'So don't expect too much action.'

'It's snooze time for me too,' Adam Hope sighed, stretching and yawning. 'Too much excitement for one day!'

Mandy's mum bundled him off to lie in the shade of a tree, then asked if she could go along as a fourth member of the team. So they set off, taking tips from Frank on how to track the bears, and spent the afternoon on hands and knees, gazing at Jack and Jill snoozing in the fork of an old oak tree from the cover of dogwood bushes.

They watched in silent fascination as Ida delicately picked caterpillars off the underside of the leaves, and gorged herself for a whole hour without stopping.

'My knees ache!' Emily Hope sat back and stretched out her legs. Ida had joined her cubs in the tree. She climbed by hugging the trunk and shinning up with her powerful back legs.

'Yes, but isn't it fantastic!' For Mandy the time had flown and she felt she was really getting to know about the habits of the three beautiful bears. She turned to Frank with yet another question. 'Why is Ida sticking around Omaha Springs when she has this long journey ahead of her? Wouldn't it make sense to set off as soon as possible?'

'In more ways than one,' James added, reminding them that the bears weren't welcome on the farm.

'She's gotta feed and rest up,' Frank told them. 'Once she starts, she won't stop. She'll travel by night and sleep by day. All the feeding she's doing now gets laid down as fat to supply her with the energy she needs for the trip.' Frank told them the bears would probably stay put in the oak tree until later that evening. Emily Hope suggested a coffee break. Reluctantly Mandy and James agreed to go back to the camp.

'Mu-um!' An idea was creeping up on Mandy in the slow, lazy heat of the afternoon. Back there in the oak tree were Ida and the cubs, soon to set out on their heroic journey. Ahead of them, she and James had one more week of holiday.

'Uh-oh. This sounds like something I'll have to think seriously about!' her mum teased. They linked arms and strolled along the riverside.

'You know it's going to be really tough for Frank to keep track of Ida all by himself?'

Mrs Hope smiled. 'You think he needs help? Frank, do *you* think you need help?'

He grinned back. 'A couple of assistants?'

James showed Mandy his crossed fingers.

'We wouldn't get in the way,' Mandy promised. 'And we'd learn ever such a lot!'

'No doubt.' The corners of Emily Hope's mouth twitched. 'A hundred and thirty miles is an awful long trek!'

'Easy!'

'What would your dad and I do while you went bear tracking?'

'Stay here.' Mandy said they could sunbathe and fish and do nothing all day long.

'I guess I could drive them back when we were through,' Frank said. 'I have to come back myself anyway, to check on Charlie Brown.'

'Hmm.'

'Does that mean yes?' Mandy urged.

'It means "Hmm".' Emily Hope wouldn't promise. 'It means I'm thinking about it, but first I'll have to talk to your dad!'

# Six

'Pinch me, someone!' James grinned like a Cheshire cat. 'Am I dreaming, or did they say yes?'

He and Mandy were sitting on the steps of the Owens' porch that evening. The air was calm and cool as they looked out over the rolling green hills that led all the way to Little Rock.

'They said we can go!' Mandy herself could hardly believe it. They were going to be Frank Crews' assistants as he followed Ida and the cubs on their trek back home.

'Frank said we need to carry a tent and a sleeping-bag, but no cooking stuff.' James got practical. 'He has all that already.'

Inside the house, the grown-ups chatted easily. Dusty and Marie Owen seemed to have calmed down again after they'd got over the disappointment of losing one of their sheep, though they still grumbled about the crazy rules regarding bears. They blamed the state authority, the tourists who fed the bears and encouraged them to scavenge from garbage cans near the houses, and of course the scientists.

Mandy stared into the distance, across the sheep-studded fields. 'All we need is for Ida to decide that it's time to go!' Now that her mum and dad had agreed to the plan, she was impatient for the bears to begin their journey.

'Maybe tomorrow morning?' James suggested.

'Or maybe tonight?' Mandy remembered that the bears liked to travel in the dark, when it was quiet. Frank had promised to call and collect them the moment there was any sign of Ida beginning to move. 'She's had loads to eat today – caterpillars, fish, berries, insects.'

They sat wondering how much longer it would be, listening to the dry, scratching chorus of the cicadas in the grass, ready to drop everything and set off at a moment's notice.

'Come on.' James stood up suddenly.

'Where to?'

'Anywhere. I hate sitting doing nothing.'

Mandy agreed. 'OK, let's go and look in on the two sheep in the barn.' She knew that Dusty Owen was hoping to put them back in the fields as soon as they were strong enough. Her mum had said they were well on the road to recovery.

So they wandered across the farmyard, past the Owens' battered pick-up truck where a couple of hens scratched and pecked at the dusty ground. A cockerel raised his green head near the barn door, ruffling his feathers, raising his red comb and squawking in annoyance as they passed.

The barn door was open, the air inside heavy with the sweet smell of stored fruit. Daylight was fading as they stepped quietly towards the wooden stall.

'*Ble-eh*!' A sheep bleated.

James stopped and looked around cautiously.

'It's OK, it's only us!' Mandy leaned over the side of the stall and looked in. The two young sheep sat in a bed of straw, their legs folded under them. They saw Mandy and stood up, tails wagging.

'Shh!' James peered into a dark corner of the barn. 'Mandy, I've got this feeling . . .'

Mandy felt the hairs on the back of her neck prickle. A feeling that someone or something else was in the gloomy barn. She listened hard.

By now James was certain. 'You stay here by the door, in case it tries to escape.' He inched towards the deep shadows.

'Be careful!' Mandy thought she heard a scrape and a shuffle; something big. Was it animal or human?

He nodded. 'I'm going to take a look around this corner!'

There was a tall wooden partition, and beyond that a stepladder leading to a loft. 'James, I'm coming too!' Mandy took her courage into her hands and followed him. The noises were coming from the high platform under the sloping roof. She recognised the sharp scrabble of claws against wooden boards. This was an animal then!

James was already halfway up the ladder. He glanced down at Mandy. 'This is the only way it can get down,' he warned. 'So watch out!'

'James, don't you think we ought to fetch someone?' In the stall below, the sheep had set up a loud alarm. Now the animal in the loft must know they were there. She pictured them coming face to face with a frightened racoon, even a fierce bobcat.

Too late. The creature, or creatures, came padding along the boards. There was a sharp

growl, heavy breaths, then a pair of small, dark glittering eyes staring down at them.

'Ida!' James grasped the ladder.

'And the cubs!' Mandy saw two smaller faces peer over the edge of the loft, their broad noses twitching, their button-eyes bright. 'What are you doing up there?'

'Stealing apples from my fruit loft, that's what!' Dusty Owen had come running at the sound of the frightened sheep. He stood framed in the open doorway, his legs wide apart, his shotgun raised and ready to fire.

'No, wait!' James yelled, almost losing his footing on the ladder. He clung on.

'What for? For them to ruin me?' The farmer steadied his aim. 'Lord knows what kind of mess they've made of my apple harvest!'

'You can't do that!' Mandy leaped to the ground, staggering as she landed. He was aiming at Ida. She ran at him to stop him from shooting.

'Mandy, get out of the way!' It was her dad's voice. More footsteps came running across the farmyard.

She ignored the warning. 'Stop him!' she pleaded.

Then she heard Ida roar. Turning again, she was just in time to see the bear leap down. She landed with a snarl, showing her pointed teeth, charging straight at the rancher and his gun.

But Mandy dived at him first, caught his arm and sent his aim awry. The gun went off with a deafening crack. There was a cry, a howl of pain, then silence.

'What's going on?' Emily Hope arrived seconds after the gun had been fired. She stood in the barn doorway, arms raised in warning at the mother bear who came charging out with one of the cubs.

'Stand back!' Adam Hope yelled. 'Let them go!'

Mandy's mum stepped quickly to one side. 'Where's the other cub?'

'In here, injured. But no one else is hurt. It's OK!'

'It's *not* OK!' Mandy cried. She picked herself up from the floor and ran for the ladder. James was up in the apple loft, bending over the injured cub.

'Take it easy.' Dusty Owen's voice rose above the panic. 'If you hadn't gotten in the way, I'd have aimed wide and missed!'

It was too late to tell them that. Mandy had reacted to save Ida's life. Now the poor little cub had taken the shot instead. 'Oh, Dad, come up here quick!' she pleaded.

'I said take it easy.' The rancher ran to the door to fire more shots after Ida and the other cub. 'These are only plastic bullets. No one's gonna die here!' The rifle cracked again. The hens in the farmyard scattered and ducked out of sight.

'Plastic bullets?' Emily Hope echoed.

'Sure. Like I said, it's all they let me use.' He lowered the gun, satisfied to see the back of the angry mother bear and one of her cubs. 'I can scare them, but I can't kill them. That's the law!'

'What about Jack?' Up in the loft, James and Mandy stood back to let Adam Hope take a look. The cub whined and cowered in a corner, too frightened to move.

'It looks like the bullet hit him. But if Dusty's using plastic bullets there'll be no wound.' He approached carefully. 'One of these can stun an animal this size pretty badly, but nothing worse.'

Mandy whispered under her breath. 'Poor little thing!'

'What do we do now?' James asked. He watched Mr Hope pick the whining, trembling cub up and make for the ladder.

'First we make sure he's OK.' Adam Hope climbed down to face Dusty Owen, showing him that the cub was dazed but probably unhurt. 'What happened to the mother?' he asked.

'Heading for the river with the other cub,' came the grudging reply. The rancher shook his head. 'Your girl got in my line of fire; that's why this happened.'

'I thought you were going to kill them!' Mandy slowly gathered her senses.

'Listen, never mind that for now.' Emily Hope stepped in. 'James, run and tell Frank what's happened. Tell him we have to get this cub back with his mother as soon as possible. He's pitched his tent just downriver from us.'

James sped off with the message.

'Won't Ida come back for him?' Mandy went up to where her father held Jack in his arms. The cub was still shaking with fear, and his eyes had glazed over with shock.

'Too dangerous,' Adam Hope told her, handing her the cub to hold. 'She probably thinks the shot was for real.'

By now, Marie Owen had reached the barn to investigate. Her normally cheerful face was lined with worry. 'Is anyone hurt?' She went from one to another until she came to Mandy and the cub. Quickly she gathered what had happened. 'You'd better get him out of here,' she advised.

'We have to wait for James to bring Frank back,'

Mandy explained. The scientist would know exactly what to do.

Marie shook her head. She took Mandy by the shoulders and turned her towards the door. 'Go now. I don't want no bears in my barn.' Her mouth set in a thin line. 'They've caused enough trouble already.'

Emily Hope nodded. 'Marie's right. You go ahead. Meet Frank halfway, it'll be quicker.'

Still dazed, but holding the bear cub tight in her arms, Mandy set off running. Jack clung on to her T-shirt for the rough journey out of the farmyard and down the slope to the river.

As she ran, Mandy tried to organise her thoughts. *Right, we'll get Frank. He'll soon track down Ida and little Jill. You'll all be together, safe and sound!* She hugged the cub to her and half-stumbled, half-jumped on to the pebbly riverbank. 'Frank's tent is down here,' she promised, murmuring under her breath to reassure the frightened animal.

'Mandy!' It was James's voice. He stood at a bend in the creek, waving with both hands.

Then Frank Crews came running with a bag slung over his shoulder. 'It's OK, James told me what happened. You did great, both of you!'

Mandy gasped with relief as she handed the cub over. 'He's scared, but Dad says he's not badly hurt.

We want you to take him back to his mother!'

'Soon,' Frank agreed. 'Don't worry about that. Ida will stick around. She won't be hard to find.' He dumped his bag on to the pebbles and unzipped it. 'But first, we're gonna do a job that'll make it real easy to track you on this big journey you've got ahead of you.' Talking gently to the cub, he took a length of black nylon webbing from the bag.

'What's that?' James crouched beside them. He was hot and out of breath, and his brown hair was plastered to his forehead.

'It's a collar with a radio transmitter in this little plastic section here.' Frank asked Mandy to hold the cub still while he slipped the collar around his neck. 'It'll transmit signals on a frequency that I can pick up on the receiver I carry in this bag.'

James nodded. 'OK, so following them when they set off is going to be dead easy.'

'*If* they set off!' Mandy was afraid that getting Jack back to Ida and Jill would be the hard thing. She felt Jack struggle. 'That shotgun scared us all stiff, Ida included. If I was her, I'd be halfway to Wolf Point by now!'

'No. A mother bear doesn't give up on her cub that easy.' Frank made sure the collar was firmly fastened. He checked the signal on the small receiver, then nodded. 'Perfect. At least one good thing came out of the bears going into the barn.'

'Can I let him go?' Mandy asked. Despite Frank's confidence, she felt they were short of time. By now the evening was drawing in, and there was no knowing for sure where Ida had fled to.

But Mandy needn't have worried. As she set Jack on his wobbly legs and watched him stagger sideways, they heard the by-now familiar sounds of someone splashing through shallow water, scrunching with heavy feet over the pebble bank.

And here they came, silhouettes in the dark evening light, padding steadily downstream. Ida and Jill ran to rescue Jack from the clutches of the enemy humans. The mother bore down on them without fear, surging through the water as she took a short-cut round a bend, baring her teeth to roar out a loud warning.

'It's OK, she won't hurt us,' Frank held Mandy and James steady. 'Don't move. You'll distract her.'

They watched as the shaky cub took his first steps to freedom. Ida warned them off with one last ear-splitting growl. Then she reached Jack and stood guard over him, licking him with her long tongue, checking to see that he was all right. Jill kept close by her side, head down, staring suspiciously at Jack's rescuers.

'She's brave!' James whispered, amazed by what the mother bear had done. She'd been shot at and hounded off the farm, yet she'd returned fearlessly to find Jack.

'She'd die for her cubs,' Frank whispered. 'Luckily this time there's no need!' He watched closely, satisfied that no harm had been done.

Mandy thought of all that the bears had been through: trapped and imprisoned by the farmers from Little Rock, dumped in hostile territory, hunted and hated, yelled at, shot at, and finally driven off. Yet here they were, back together. Whatever anyone did to them, they couldn't force them apart. 'She's wonderful!' Mandy caught Ida's gaze. She read courage in that look. 'She won't let anyone beat her!'

'You bet.' Frank packed his bag. 'Now go and get your things,' he told them.

James and Mandy stood flat-footed, open-mouthed.

'I thought you two planned to come along?' Frank said as he strapped his bag round his shoulders. He took a cap out of his pocket and set it firmly on his head. 'Is your stuff packed?'

Mandy jerked into action. 'You mean, we're actually setting off?' She scrambled upstream along the bank, as Ida and the cubs lifted their heads and sniffed the air. They turned this way and that, tested the wind, and listened.

Frank nodded. 'Sure thing.'

James followed Mandy, running for his rucksack. 'Wait for us!' he pleaded over his shoulder.

'I'll give you five minutes.' The scientist stood with his back to them, carefully checking the signal he was receiving on the radio. 'That's all you got. Ida ain't gonna hang around waiting for you two to pack your sleeping-bags!'

Mandy ran. They had to collect their things, tell her mum and dad, and get back to Frank as quick as they could. 'This is it!' she whispered to James.

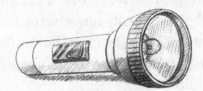

# *Seven*

It was dark when Ida began her journey home. The moon was full and bright in a clear, starlit sky.

'I guess she'll stick to the creek until she reaches White Rock River.' Frank plotted her course by the water's edge.

James stopped to study the map by torchlight. 'What happens when they reach Oakville?' It looked like a big town in the fork where the two rivers met.

'She'll keep right on,' Frank promised. 'That'll be tomorrow night. She'll find a den and rest the cubs when it gets light. The town won't send her off course, she'll just keep on trucking!' He turned to Mandy. 'How are your feet holding up?'

It was three o'clock in the morning. They'd been travelling for almost five hours. 'Feet are OK, legs hurt.' Mandy had hardly any energy to reply. Ida was setting a fast pace, forcing them to jog to keep up. 'Don't these bears ever need a rest?'

'Not until daybreak.'

'I thought we'd see more of them,' James said. So far, they'd had only a couple of sightings: once when they spotted Ida and the cubs standing on a rocky ledge that overhung the creek, once slipping like shadows across an open farmyard. For the rest of the time, they'd relied on the radio tag and the tiny bleep on Frank's receiver to tell them exactly where the bears were headed.

'Hold it!' Frank gave the order to halt as the radio beeps bunched together in rapid pips. 'Looks like they did take a break after all. I reckon they're down in that hollow.' He pointed to a wooded slope close to the fast running water. The slope ended in the pale white glow of limestone cliffs falling steeply to the creek.

'Ha!' Mandy stopped and bent double to catch her breath. This was harder work than she'd expected. But the breather gave her the chance to look and listen. Overhead, the stars were clear pinpricks of light in a dark blue canopy. On the jagged horizon, black hills rose and fell. 'I never thought it'd be this noisy!' she murmured, standing with her hands on her hips, and her head back.

In the trees where the bears were resting, a screech-owl shrieked. Small creatures rustled through the grass, heard but not seen.

'Why have they stopped?' James wanted to know.

'Could be they've found food,' Frank guessed. He marked his own map to show how far they'd travelled. 'Thirty miles in just under five hours,' he told them. Then he glanced up. 'No, forget the food. There's your reason.' He pointed beyond the trees where Ida had taken shelter, to an empty hillside. The silver moonlight picked out the clear shape of a bear. 'This is home territory for a male called Arnie.'

'Is he part of your programme?' Mandy watched the bear trundle up the slope. He rocked from side to side as he walked, brushing through a patch of bushes, and planting his broad feet squarely on the earth. 'Does he have a radio tag?'

'Yep.' Frank changed the frequency on the receiver to pick up a steady *beep-beep*. 'That's Arnie's signal; it's a different rhythm to the one we put on Jack. Listen.'

They nodded.

'Arnie's moving upwind of Ida, so he couldn't pick up her scent.' Frank explained that a bear's sense of smell was especially strong. 'See what he's doing now?'

They watched the bear suddenly stop and roll on to his back, legs in the air. Then he picked himself up and trotted on.

'That's him telling everyone that this is his patch,' Frank explained. 'He's marking his territory. And you hear that noise he's making?'

Mandy picked up a distant, muffled coughing sound. 'Is that a warning?'

'Yep. It means, "Don't mess with me!" '

'Who'd dare?' James was impressed by the male bear's size and strength.

'Would he attack Ida if he knew she was there?' Mandy pictured her with her cubs, hidden deep in the wood.

Frank nodded. 'These are highly territorial animals, remember.'

So they waited in anxious silence, relieved when Arnie had marked a few trees with his claws, rolled on the ground again, then plodded on over the crest of the hill at last. He hadn't picked up any sign that Ida was there. But minutes had ticked by; valuable journey time had been lost.

Then the radio signal told them that Ida was on the move again, and they even glimpsed the three bears creep silently out of the wood, keeping low in the valley out of harm's way. They were off, covering the ground before day broke. As the first streaks of pinkish-grey appeared in the east, they crossed Bear Creek at a shallow point where a farm track forded the stream.

'Wet feet,' Frank warned, plunging knee-deep after the bears.

Mandy forced herself to follow, cringing at the cold water, feeling it swirl around her legs. *If Jack and Jill can do it, so can I!* she thought.

But she came up the far bank soaked and weary,

longing for the dawn. 'Why did they need to cross the river?' she gasped.

Frank showed her on the map. 'Draw a straight line between Omaha Springs and Mount Ida, and it crosses Bear Creek right here.'

'She's dead on course!' James agreed.

'And I'm dead tired!' Mandy's legs felt weak and wobbly. She saw now why Ida and the cubs had spent days building up their strength.

Then, as the sun rose at last, the radio signal told them that the bears were slowing down. They were on fenced land, close to a farmhouse, but that didn't seem to put them off. As Frank, James and Mandy waited at a safe distance, the dawn light showed them Ida scouting around the back of the farm buildings by herself. She nosed into a shed and under the parked truck, checked out a pond in a hollow where ducks swam, then padded back up to investigate a barn.

'Oh no!' Mandy groaned. The memory of what had happened to the bears in Dusty Owen's barn was all too fresh. 'Let's stop her!'

Mandy was all for rushing forward to warn the bears away. But Frank caught her arm and explained. 'No way. That's not part of what we do.' He watched through narrowed eyes as Ida nosed open one section of the wide wooden door and gingerly stepped inside.

'Why not?' James couldn't figure it out. 'Isn't it dangerous for her to rest inside a barn?'

'Could be. But our job is to stay clear. What we're doing is recording the details of what these bears have to do to get back to Mount Ida. That means no interference, OK?'

'But what if the farmer finds them?' Mandy couldn't see the sense. Her fears eased when the mother bear came padding silently out of the barn, but they grew again when she saw her return minutes later with the cubs in tow.

'There's nothing we can do,' Frank insisted. 'We ruin the study if we move in to help them. Ida's the one in charge here.' He smiled sympathetically at his two helpers.

'And can't we even tell the farmer what's going on?' James suggested. 'You know, say there's a mother bear and two cubs using his barn as a den for the day, so that he doesn't do what Mr Owen did?'

Frank thought about it. 'What if this guy doesn't like bears either? It's even likely that Mr Owen has been ringing round all the ranches to warn them about Ida.'

Mandy knew that the Owens had it in for the 'nuisance' bear. She agreed. 'Yes, and this farmer might use real bullets!' Better not to take the risk.

'So let's hope Ida finds a good spot to hide in there,' James said quietly. It was clear that she'd found a resting place that suited her. Now all they could do was wait.

'Trust her. She knows what she's doing.' Frank was busy choosing his own spot. He unrolled his sleeping-bag under a huge oak tree outside the fence that ran along the boundary of the farm. He set the radio receiver carefully on a flat stone next to him. Its steady, muffled beep would as ever keep him in touch with the bears.

Mandy and James copied him, choosing flat ground between the twisting, gnarled roots to catch up on some sleep. They took off their damp boots and hung their socks over a low branch to dry. Then, leaving the rest of their clothes on, they snuggled into their bags.

'This is weird!' James whispered. 'Going to bed when it's getting light.'

Mandy lay on her back, staring up into the leaves. 'I could sleep on a bed of nails!' Except that she was still worried. 'Another barn, of all places!' she sighed. Her mind wandered; the sound of rustling leaves filled her head as the sky slowly turned from grey to blue and the stars faded.

Something clicked. 'Stars!' she said suddenly,

propping herself on her elbows. 'I bet that's how they do it!'

Silence from James.

'James – the bears – the stars . . . they find their way home by following the stars!' It was simple and amazing at the same time. Mandy felt like she'd taken a magic key and unlocked the mystery of the bears' amazing homing instinct.

'James – Frank – I know how Ida does it!'

Silence again. Except for the bleep of the radio and a chorus of steady, soft snores from her two weary companions.

'There goes your theory!' James whispered, as Ida, Jack and Jill woke from their daytime sleep and hit the trail once more.

The bears had spent the day in the safety of the strange barn and crept out as dusk fell. The radio signal told Frank that they were on the move.

Mandy had carefully explained her idea about how the bears could use the stars to plot their route back to Little Rock. She'd woken in the late afternoon, then helped Frank to prepare a supper of soup, bread, cheese and fruit. For a time she'd managed to convince James that she'd come up with a brilliant solution. 'Ida recognises the pattern of the stars in the sky. All she has to do is follow them until she gets back home!'

'Like honey-bees find their hive by following the angle of the sun?' He'd considered it carefully. 'It sounds unbelievably brilliant!'

But Frank had just listened, shrugged and got on with his supper. Now Mandy could see why.

'No stars,' James pointed out a sky covered with thick clouds, as Ida crept out of the barn, coaxing the cubs to stay close. A chestnut-coloured horse in a field behind the barn kicked up his heels and galloped away. Inside the house, a dog barked.

Mandy couldn't argue. She stared up at the darkening clouds. She had to admit that the gathered clouds hid every single star. Yet Ida never hesitated. She led her cubs up the hill away from the farm, keeping to the invisible, arrow-straight line between Omaha Springs and Little Rock.

'Nice idea,' Frank told her. 'Neat to think that bears are like sailors way back, navigating by the stars. Only, like James says, Ida doesn't need a clear sky to find her way.' He shouldered his rucksack, ready to follow. 'It must be something else. You guys got waterproof jackets?'

They nodded and fished them out of their bags.

'You're gonna need them tonight.'

Warm, soft drops of rain had begun to fall before they even got clear of the ranch. The dog inside the house kept on barking, and a man came out to investigate. He leaned on the rail of his porch and scanned the hillsides, catching sight of Mandy, James and Frank as they skirted the field with the chestnut horse. He yelled at them, got into his truck and rode across the field to join them.

'Uh-oh, let's keep going!' James thought that if they got a move on, they could reach the cover of some pine trees before the farmer caught up. He'd sounded angry, determined to find out what they were up to.

'No, we should wait,' Frank decided.

'What about Ida? She'll be miles away if we get held up,' Mandy said.

'That's where the radio tag comes in.' Frank knew that the signal would keep them on the right track. 'This guy looks like he really wants to talk!'

The farmer was hanging out of the side window as he drove his truck up the hill. A German shepherd sat alongside him and leaped out as soon as he stopped. The dog came bounding towards them ahead of the man.

'Good boy, stay down!' Mandy could tell by the wag of his tail that he was friendly, even if his master wasn't. He sat and she patted his neck, waiting for the farmer's interrogation to begin.

'Are you Frank Crews?' The farmer didn't

bother with greetings, just strode across their path and stood with his hands on his hips. He was a grey-haired man with a dark moustache, wearing a red checked shirt and jeans.

'That's me.' Frank's gaze didn't waver. 'I work for the State Parks Bear Program.'

'Yeah, yeah. I spoke on the phone to Dusty Owen.'

Mandy bit her lip and glanced at James. Frank had been right; the angry rancher had been warning his neighbours about Ida.

'I'm Johnny Marlowe. You must be the two British kids?' He ignored the rain as he waited for an answer.

James nodded warily. 'We're helping Frank.'

'Sure. You're tracking a family of bears down-river. I heard about it. It sounds crazy to me, but I guess if that's what you wanna do . . .' He shrugged.

'You're not throwing us off your land?' Mandy was puzzled. What had brought the rancher chasing them up the hillside? She was still looking for a loaded shotgun hidden inside the truck.

'Nope. I got a message from Dusty for you. It don't make a whole lot of sense to me; he said to tell you Ida is not guilty!'

'Wow!' James made them jump. He blushed and stepped forward. 'What else did he say?'

'Not a thing. Wouldn't tell me what was going on. Just said to give you the message if you passed my way. Said for you to give him a call.' The rancher turned on his heel with a sharp call to his dog.

Mandy ran after him. 'When was this? How long ago?'

'Midday. "Ida's not guilty!" That was it; the full message.' The gleam in his grey eyes wasn't unfriendly. 'You're Mandy? Dusty said he reckoned you'd specially want to know.'

She nodded and grinned. 'Thanks.'

'You want to call from my place?'

'If there's time.' She turned to ask Frank, who nodded.

'I'll wait here,' he promised.

So Mandy and James set off in the truck with Johnny Marlowe. The rough ride was over in a couple of minutes, then he was showing them into the house, dialling Omaha Springs and handing the phone to Mandy without another word. He went off to feed his dog in the kitchen while they made the call.

'He doesn't say much, does he?' James stood by, staring around the bare hallway. There were boots kicked off into a corner, ropes lassoed around a set of coat hooks, and a denim jacket slung across a chair.

'No, but he seems OK.' Mandy waited for the Owens to answer their phone. When a voice came on the line, however, it turned out to be her mum.

'Hi, Mandy. We've been waiting for you to get in touch. Did you hear the news?'

'Mum! Ida's not guilty. That's what Mr Marlowe's told us. What's it mean?'

'It means you're not to worry any more about Dusty accusing Ida of attacking his sheep,' she explained, calm and unhurried as ever. 'We've found out that it's not her.'

'How come? What happened to change his mind?' Mandy tried to fill James in with the news as she listened. 'She says they know what's been attacking Dusty's sheep!' she whispered.

'We caught the culprit in the act late this morning. It's a bobcat.'

'Yes!' She clenched her fist. 'Where?'

'Below Wolf Point. I was up there with Dusty. We actually saw it happen. The bobcat was hidden in a tree, waiting for the lamb to come within reach. We were a little way away, so he didn't hear us. He jumped right on top of the lamb from up above ... The lamb wouldn't have stood a chance if we hadn't been there ... As it happened, he didn't have time to sink his teeth into the poor thing's neck before we chased him off. And there was the evidence right in front of Dusty's eyes!'

'How's the lamb?' Mandy had gabbled the story to James during the pauses.

'She's in the barn with the other two casualties. But she didn't lose much blood. The wounds on her neck aren't deep. She should be fine.' There was another, longer pause 'Dusty and Marie feel bad about blaming the bear. They want to know if there's anything they can do to help.'

'Tell them it's OK, Mum.' She was glad the truth had come out at last. 'Say thanks to them for letting us know.'

'So no hard feelings?'

'No. I can't really blame them for thinking it could be Ida.'

'Good girl, Mandy. I'll tell them you said thanks.'

'And say hi to Dad from me.'

'I will. Hey, guess who he saw early this morning?'

'Charlie Brown?' Mandy guessed.

'Yep. As close as anything. Your dad took photos.'

'Lucky Dad.'

'We're thinking about you. How are you getting on?'

'Fine.' Mandy thought of the long, wet night ahead, the hills they would have to climb, and the farms and towns they would have to pass through. Suddenly, a cosy night in the tent in their sheltered bend in the river, waking up to breakfast with her mum and dad, seemed like paradise.

Emily Hope's voice came down the line. 'I'd better let you go now. And don't worry, there'll be no angry ranchers after Ida's blood after all.'

'Thanks, Mum. Bye!'

'Bye, love. Take care!'

Putting the phone down was hard. But Mandy knew every minute was precious.

James stood at the door. 'Time to track those bears,' he said quietly, as they stepped out into the rain.

# *Eight*

*Saturday. 2 am Oakville.* Frank jotted details in his notebook. *Ida and the cubs have picked up speed. Twenty-five miles in two hours. They hit town an hour ago. Heavy rainfall. No sign of let-up in the bears' speed as they head south.*

Johnny Marlowe leaned out of his truck to shake hands with Frank. 'This is as far as I go. I've got sheep to bring down from the hills at my place later today.' The windscreen wipers swished to and fro, and the wet sidewalks gleamed.

'It's good of you to bring us this far,' Frank told him.

'We'd never have kept up with Ida otherwise,' Mandy added.

After the phone call to her mum, Johnny had told James and Mandy to hop in the truck. He'd driven them to meet up with Frank, then offered to drive them along the rough forest road. For half the night he had helped them to track the bears.

'No problem,' Johnny said with a grin. 'But I still think you're all crazy!'

Mandy leaned in to stroke his obedient dog, who sat up front beside Johnny. 'We probably are. But thanks for everything!'

He nodded, then reversed the truck, gave a wave and set off for home. They stood in the rain, watching the brake lights glow red, then disappear around a corner of the quiet suburban street.

'He was nice.' Mandy sighed, wishing that he could have stayed with them all the way to Little Rock. It gave her hope that with ranchers like Johnny Marlowe in the area, bears like Arnie and Charlie Brown stood a good chance of surviving for a long time in the mountains of Arkansas.

'Ida's on the move!' It was James who brought them back to earth. He listened to the radio and told Frank that the bleeps had altered. 'Let's go.'

They followed the signal down the long, curving

drive on the outskirts of town, catching glimpses of the three bears in the gardens of large white houses, crossing parking lots beside supermarkets, and plodding on through more housing estates.

'If only the people asleep in their beds knew they had bears in their gardens!' Mandy grinned.

James agreed. 'Who's been swinging on *my* swing? Who's been eating *my* muesli?' he boomed, then laughed.

Joking let them forget the heavy tiredness in their legs, and the rain that soaked through their trousers and trickled down the backs of their necks.

Meanwhile, magnificent Ida plodded on, past postboxes that lined the roadside, through pools of orange light cast by streetlights, across minor roads, towards the distant roar of traffic on the interstate highway. And all the time, the two cubs trotted quietly beside their mother, one on either side, keeping pace, never letting up.

'Anyway, it's a good job they don't realise the bears are here. They'd die of shock!' James had been given the job of checking the radio receiver while Frank kept on making notes. They'd lost sight of the bears in the playground of a junior high school, but he signalled the way to go. 'Down here!'

They crossed the playground into an area of shops and restaurants. Behind that, the highway lights glowed.

Mandy felt herself grow tense. Though it was the middle of the night, there was steady traffic out there. The town came to an abrupt end and there was a band of rough ground, then a bank beside the road, lined with tall billboards and neon signs advertising drinks, cafes and motels.

They came to a halt and stood at the top of the bank, staring down at the giant trucks roaring along the highway. 'Do the bears have to cross this?' she whispered to Frank.

He nodded, then listened in to the signal. 'But right now Ida's taking the cubs along the bank on this side.'

'Maybe she's looking for a safe place to cross,' James said.

'No such thing.' Mandy felt the knot in her stomach tighten as she scanned the bank for a sign of the bears. On the highway below, the trucks thundered past. Suddenly the hazards that Ida and her cubs had faced on their journey so far – angry farmers and hostile male bears – seemed small by comparison. Mandy sensed she was standing there helpless, staring into the dark and the rain, waiting for something terrible to happen.

Another truck sped by, gleaming silver. Its giant tyres sprayed water high up the bank. 'Frank, what are we going to do?' Mandy cried. If only they could spot Ida, find out what was happening, and try to help her across the nightmare highway.

'Nothing.' He reminded them of the rule. 'We keep our distance. No stepping in to help.'

'What could we do anyway?' James said, his face tense as he crouched over the radio. 'Nothing's going to stop this traffic!'

Two more wagons roared by, their headlights glaring. The highway was straight and wide. The drivers in their high cabs took it fast, driving through the night.

'Oh no, look!' Mandy spotted Ida first. Like them, she stood at the top of the bank, staring down at the highway. The cubs huddled between her front legs, trying to shelter from the noise and the rain. They were a few hundred metres down the road, half hidden by the forest of billboards.

James, Frank and Mandy froze. For a moment, Mandy had a mad urge to run down and stop the traffic. She could stand at the roadside, flag the trucks down and make a safe gap for the bears to cross. But it was too late even to do this, because Ida had set off down the bank, head down, defying

the hideous roar and the waves of spray. She urged her cubs ahead of her, determined to go on.

James turned his head away. 'I can't look!'

The bears had reached the hard shoulder of the dual carriageway. Now they were caught in the headlights' glare as a truck sped by. Then darkness drowned them, then there was another set of headlights, another monstrous engine roar, and a whirl of slipstream. Darkness again, and the choking fumes as Ida and her cubs teetered on the brink.

'Please let them be safe!' Mandy whispered.

Frank held his arm up to shield his face from

the spray, and perhaps to hide the fear in his own eyes. James forced himself to turn and look.

*Waa-ah*! A small truck blared its horn, then swerved out of the inside lane as its headlights caught the shape of the bears stepping out on to the highway. The driver slammed on the brakes, skidded, then carried straight on. Behind him, the driver of one of the monster trucks drove wide into the fast lane.

Ida turned her head to look for oncoming traffic.

'Don't stop!' James whispered, urging her on.

Another truck was coming. Its headlights raked along the central reservation, the sound of its engine drawing near.

'Keep going!' Mandy felt sick in her stomach. What chance did a bear have against tons of speeding metal?

The truck turned the bend and its headlights glared. Ida and the cubs gazed into them, transfixed. Then, as the truck bore down, Ida raised herself on to her hind legs in a futile challenge. The cubs cowered against her. The machine hurtled on.

*Whoo-oosh*! The driver saw the bears and steered on to the hard shoulder. Wheels churned through puddles, brake lights glowed, then the truck swerved back on to the main carriageway.

'What happened? Did he hit them?' James's voice quivered as they stared down at the highway.

'No. They're OK!' Mandy breathed again.

Ida was down on all fours, urging the cubs on to the central reservation. For a few moments, at least, they were safe.

But one of the cubs broke away in terror. The lights and thundering machines had made him forget the first rule, to stay close to his mother at all times. Now he ran down the central strip of grass, trying to hide in a cluster of sparse bushes growing there.

What would Ida do? There was less traffic on the far carriageway. The gaps between the terrifying headlights were longer. She decided to take one cub across and come back for the other. Quickly she seized her chance.

'That's Jill,' James whispered as they saw the first cub arrive at the far side of the highway. 'She's not wearing a collar. It must have been Jack who ran away.'

Frank signalled for them to move along the bank for a better view. 'Now she's coming back for him.' He pointed to where the frightened cub had hidden amongst the bushes.

The danger continued, for though the female

cub stayed obediently on the far bank, Ida had to face the lights and the thundering trucks once more. They came steadily, appearing out of the darkness, making the whole world rumble and flash.

But the bear bravely went back for her second cub. She waited until the lights had died, then, under cover of the blackness in between, she ran to fetch him, dragging him out of his hiding-place by the scruff of his neck, and badgering him across the carriageway before the next truck appeared. The little bear cowered and scuttled, then ran whimpering up the bank to his sister. Their mother followed. The traffic was safely behind them now, and open country stretched out ahead.

Silence. The lights on the highway were miles behind, the rain had stopped. Under the dark sky, Ida led her family on. Only now had the knot in Mandy's stomach eased; it was the fear of the giant trucks that could so easily have crushed the bears to death.

'It's nearly dawn,' Frank promised, stopping to wait for her at the summit of a hill. He shone his torch on the map to show her that they'd covered half the journey to Little Rock. 'And no more major highways to cross.' He listed the good news.

'Thanks to Johnny Marlowe we're managing to keep up. The study is working out really well.'

Mandy nodded, seeing that the bears had kept to an absolutely straight line on the map. 'We've got loads of evidence about Ida's homing instinct.'

'All the data we need.' Frank's energy had kept them going throughout the night. 'And it's downhill from here for a good stretch.' He showed her the dawn creeping into the valley ahead, then turned to encourage James, who trailed after Mandy.

She stood at the top of the hill, watching the grey mists swirl between the dark trees, out of the valley towards the summit. She could make out clearings, farm buildings, and hills rolling endlessly towards the horizon where a slice of pale golden sun had appeared. Soon the bears would find a place to rest. Soon the humans would be able to sleep.

'Jack seems to have stopped somewhere in this first patch of trees,' James told her, coming alongside to let her listen to the radio signal. He heaved a sigh. 'It's nowhere near a farm, so at least we won't have to worry about barns and farmers turfing them out today.'

'That just leaves other bears, picnickers, campers, hunters with permits to shoot bears . . .'

Frank was only half joking as he came to locate the bears' exact position. 'Let's not kid ourselves it's gonna be easy from here on in.'

'Hunters with permits?' James echoed. This was the first they'd heard of it.

'Sure. They come across the state line from Missouri.' Frank came out with facts and figures which they found hard to believe. 'The mortality rate for adult bears is low. In other words, bears have very few natural enemies in the wild. Fewer than five per cent die of anything other than old age. But the human threat is high. Of those five in a hundred, most are shot by hunters.' He waited for Mandy and James to come in with questions, but they were too stunned by what he was telling them.

Instead, he went on. 'OK, try to figure this: we have half a million black bears in North America. We have to cull a certain number every spring and fall . . .'

This time James did interrupt. 'That doesn't make sense! I thought the idea was to put bears back into the wild.'

'Round here that's what we do. Ida, Arnie, Charlie Brown – they're part of an endangered species in the south-east. But I'm talking about states in the north-west. There it's different.'

'So you were kidding about hunters with permits in Arkansas?' Mandy wanted to be sure. She checked the radio signal to make sure that Jack had stayed in one place since they began to talk.

'Luckily.' Frank checked the rising sun and decided it was safe to put down their rucksacks and make camp. 'It looks like they're making a den for the day.' He seemed satisfied with Ida's choice. 'Plenty of ground cover,' he pointed out. 'They may even decide to have some berries for breakfast before they rest up. Talking of breakfast . . .' He unpacked the tiny stove and set a pan of water to boil, while Mandy eased her shoulders and peered down the slope into the valley.

The sun was rising and there was more light. Colour crept into the landscape: the dark green of pine trees, and patches of yellow corn. Nearer to camp, she could see the mist rising clear of the lush green hillside, and hear the raindrops from last night patter from leaf to leaf. And there, at the edge of the woods, were Jack and Jill playing in full view.

'Did you see that?' James pointed to the two honey-coloured cubs. His voice carried downhill and they scampered out of sight.

Mandy nodded. 'I wonder where Ida is.' She

scanned the slope. Dawn had brought a loud chorus of birdsong and the usual scurrying back and forth amongst the bushes. But the mother bear was nowhere to be seen.

'Fetching berries, I expect.' James sat down on the ground to enjoy the cubs as they came cheekily into view again. This was the reward for an exhausting and terrifying night's trek – to watch the cubs at play.

First Jack spotted a young, slender pine tree. He shinned up it with ease, bending the trunk with his weight. Then he sat swaying near the top. He held on as Jill followed him up the trunk. The tree bent until it threatened to break. Suddenly Jill jumped to the ground. The tree trunk sprang back, catapulting Jack in a wild arc through the air as he clung on tight.

Mandy and James grinned at their game. When the tree stopped swaying, Jack jumped to the ground and it was Jill's turn. They kept on, taking it in turns until Ida came back through the forest, limping slightly, lumbering up to cuff the cubs for their unwary game, and ordering them into the cover of the fully grown trees.

'Aah!' Mandy was sorry to see them go. But it was time to sleep. Somewhere in the forest there would be a tall woodpile, a stack of brushwood that would make an ideal den. The sun would bring Sunday picnickers to the hills, but Ida and the cubs would stay well hidden.

Weary and soaked to the skin from the night's adventure, but for the time being satisfied that the bears were safe, James and Mandy went to join Frank for a breakfast of bread, honey and hot, sweet tea.

# *Nine*

Walk, eat, sleep and walk. By Monday morning, Mandy knew the routine inside out.

'Altogether we've covered over a hundred miles,' James told her. On Sunday night they'd followed the bears across two narrow creeks through high limestone gorges. The rolling hillsides had turned rough and craggy; straggly trees clung to white cliff faces and rapid streams rushed over black, volcanic rock.

' "Monday. 8 am. Black Rock shut-in." ' Mandy read the last note Frank had made in his book as she sat dangling her bare feet in the ice-cold water. Ida and the cubs had broken their journey at dawn and sought shelter in a dark, dry cave.

'What's a shut-in?' James asked, putting away the map.

'It's what Mandy's got her feet in.' Frank was arranging his sleeping-bag. He pointed to the narrow stretch of river cutting its way through the rock. 'It's where the water comes up against hard rock. You get waterfalls and rapids.'

'I don't care what it's called. It feels great!' Mandy sighed. Her feet were aching and sore, like the rest of her. She leaned back against a smooth rock. 'Do you think Ida knows where she is yet?'

Frank stopped arranging his bed for a moment. 'This is still way beyond her normal home range at Mount Ida,' he said slowly. 'We're twenty-five miles away. But I guess she could start recognising landmarks any time now.'

'Can we see the mountain from here?' James grew excited. Suddenly the end of the journey was real. He climbed on to a rock for a better view of the wooded hillsides below.

'Nope.' Frank did his best to dampen the mood. He was a scientist; it wasn't his job to jump ahead, but to take one thing at a time. 'How about getting some sleep?' he advised.

'Did you notice how much Ida was limping last

night?' Mandy hardly seemed to hear. 'It's definitely got worse!'

'She can't put much weight on one of her front feet,' James agreed.

'I expect it's a thorn, or something else sharp that's got into the soft pad. Nothing too serious.'

'We hope. Anyway, she's not letting it slow her down.' James reminded Mandy how far they'd travelled.

'Yes, but they're looking pretty ragged and thin.' Mandy's mood swung rapidly between hope and fear. On the one hand, she knew how brave and determined the bears were as they trekked homewards. On the other hand, disaster could still strike. 'The cubs especially. What if they're not strong enough to make it?'

'Don't even think about it.' Wearily James went and unrolled his own sleeping-bag. 'Look, Mandy, there's probably only one more night to go, two at the most. They've got this far, haven't they?'

'But they might be too hungry and weak. They're only young!'

'Ida knows what she's doing. Trust her.' He crept into the soft, warm covering and zipped himself safely inside.

'But—' she began.

'Mandy!'

'OK.' Taking her feet out of the water, Mandy stood up to take one last look at the upstream cave which the bears had chosen as their den for the day.

Its entrance was a dark arch partly hidden by saplings, set back from the creek and surrounded by smooth white boulders. All seemed quiet in the fresh morning light.

But then Mandy saw a movement in one of the small trees. There was an animal up there, in amongst the leaves. It was leaving rapidly, scuttling down to earth.

'Racoon!' she breathed.

James and Frank took no notice, so she scrambled up the hill alone for a closer look at the furry grey animal with his striped tail and little black hands that gripped the branches as he swung to the ground. He saw her and whipped around, leaping across rocks on to a fallen tree trunk that spanned the creek. Balancing like a tightrope walker, with his tail streaming behind, he sped across.

Mandy smiled. Racoons were cheeky, quick, clever creatures peering through black markings that made a mask round their bright eyes. But what had made this one run?

*Chuff-chuff*! There was a noise from deep inside

the cave. It sounded like a chesty cough, followed by a low growl. 'Ida!' It was the noise she made when she called the cubs. 'Why aren't you asleep?' Mandy risked creeping closer to take a look. She found hand- and footholds in the steep rock that led to the entrance of the cave and began to haul herself up.

Whatever had disturbed the racoon had upset Ida too. Mandy could still hear her growling and scuffling inside the cave. Dry twigs snapped underfoot as the cubs and the mother bear paced up and down. At last Mandy climbed level with the entrance and took a good look round.

She was on a narrow ledge that ran for a hundred metres along a cliff face. It was wide enough to stand safely, with the cave worn into the rock at the end which overlooked the creek. At the other end, the ledge seemed to vanish in a sheer drop. There was nothing here to disturb the bears.

But then Mandy looked up. Shock almost made her step over the ledge and fall backwards. She waved her arms to keep her balance, reached out and grabbed hold of a twisted tree root to save herself. There, not five metres away, peering down at her from a higher ledge, was a black bear.

He crouched, ready to leap, fangs bared, his eyes fixed on her. Then he snorted.

Mandy held her breath; her heart was thumping wildly. What should she do? This creature was truly angry. He reached out an enormous paw and swatted the air. He chomped his jaws and snarled. Inside the cave, Ida returned a warning snarl.

Mandy stared back at the bear. His fur was jet black against the white limestone rock. A wide ruff of long hair around his neck made him look huge and fierce, and the inside of his mouth was pink, his teeth sharp. Mandy had never been this close to a bear before. Scared yet fascinated, she judged her next move.

'Don't turn your back on him!' It was Frank, shouting from below. The snarling must have woken him. 'Whatever you do, Mandy, keep your eye on him. If you turn away, he could attack!'

So she froze on the ledge, willing herself to meet the angry bear's gaze. To one side, the ledge fell away sharply, so she clutched the tree root and prayed for the courage to stay put.

'Good!' Frank and James were advancing up the slope.

The bear swatted his paw against the rock this time, sending sharp stones hurtling on to the ledge.

Mandy dodged them and gritted her teeth when one hit her shoulder.

'I know he looks fierce, but he's probably only bluffing!' Frank tried to give her the right instructions. 'He's young, what we call a sub-adult. He's showing off in front of Ida. What you have to do is call his bluff!'

'How do I do that?' Every nerve in Mandy's body was stretched taut. Inside the cave, she could hear the family of bears grow more and more restless.

'You have to yell and look as if you're going to advance on him!'

Mandy drew a deep breath. 'But I can't even move!' The ledge was too narrow, the way up too sheer. The black bear leaned over the edge and snarled down at her.

'See if you can let go of the tree. That's good. Now, try waving your arms!'

Mandy did as she was told. Lifting her arms above her head, she tried to shoo the bear off.

He drew back, shied away sideways, then reappeared, snarling as before.

'Again!' James yelled. 'Try shouting at him!'

She waved a second time. 'Go away!' she warned. 'Go on, shoo!' Not for a moment did she think her feeble threat would work against the massive creature who faced her.

But Frank's tactics were right. The bear didn't like her wildly waving arms or her loud voice. His head disappeared from the ledge, and this time it didn't come back. Mandy heard his feet rattle against loose stones as he retreated, and caught a glimpse of his hairy side as he turned to climb away.

'You did it!' James told her. He saw the bear heading off, its feet pounding the slope, sending stones sliding towards the ledge.

Mandy let out a loud breath and hung her head. *Scary*!

But there was more to come. Inside the cave, Ida must have heard the black bear's retreat. She seized her own chance and hurtled out of the entrance on to the ledge where Mandy still stood. Jack and Jill scrambled out after her. The three of them advanced together.

Mandy was face to face with Ida: a pale brown head with dark eyes, a weary look from a mother bear driven to the point of exhaustion. Mandy didn't feel the least bit scared. She put out a hand to help.

Ida stared at her. The cubs stayed in her shadow, waiting for her to react.

'It's OK. I won't harm you.'

The bear tilted her head to one side.

'I'm your friend.'

Ida shifted her weight and snorted. The sore

place on her front foot made her whine with pain.

'Leave her, Mandy. Come down!' Frank's voice drifted up to the ledge. 'Remember our rule!'

She was not allowed to help. Ida had to make it home by herself. 'She's hurt her foot!' Mandy called back.

'I know. But we ruin the whole study if you move in now. Days of work, all for nothing!'

'It's cruel!' She longed to ease the pain of Ida's foot, to help the mother and cubs in the last part of their journey.

'She's tough. She can make it!' Frank was pleading with her not to interfere.

But Mandy couldn't bring herself to turn her back. She crouched low and held out her arms to Jill.

Then Ida took the decision for herself. She reared up and turned round, made the cubs follow. She was picking her way down from the ledge, turning away from the shelter of the cave and Mandy's offer of help.

'Where are you going?' she cried.

The mother bear ignored her. With Mount Ida almost in sight, with their strength running out, and knowing that the young black bear would soon be back, she had decided not to sleep that day after all. They would go on.

Down from the ledge, plunging into the creek, crossing the shut-in on to the far bank, the bears began the final leg of their journey.

All that day, James, Mandy and Frank trailed far behind. They used the radio signal to track the bears, but didn't catch another glimpse of them after the scare on the ledge. It was all they could do to put one foot in front of another, forcing themselves on towards the mountain range which was Ida and the cubs' true home.

'That black bear, is he tagged?' James had tried to find out more soon after they'd set off. Since the intruder had run off, they'd seen no sign of him.

'No. He's new to the area.' Frank had taken the lead along a gloomy track through pine trees. To either side the trunks grew so close together that the sunlight was blocked. 'These sub-adults leave their mothers round this time of year and strike out for themselves. Maybe he came up from the south.' He'd sounded worried and tired.

'Is that bad?'

'Could be. I'd feel happier if we knew where he was now. You see, these new youngsters have to find a home range for themselves, one where there's plenty of food, not too many people, and definitely no other bears. If they try to settle on a rival's home range, there's a fight and one could get killed.'

Mandy had listened, but hardly took in what Frank said. Talk of home ranges, young males who fought for territory and killed any rival young males had drifted in one ear and out of the other. It was all she could do to keep on walking. Her eyelids drooped, she plodded on.

Eventually they'd reached the top of a ridge and found a new horizon. There was a green valley, a blue lake. The sky was cloudless in the afternoon heat.

James had been studying the map since midday, plotting the last leg of Ida's journey. Now he took it out and drew another tiny cross. He looked up and with narrowed eyes he scanned the hazy blue hills. 'Mount Ida,' he said quietly, reaching out and pointing.

Mandy shaded her eyes. The mountain was a perfect pyramid in the distance. The lake lay sparkling at its foot. Mount Ida. Journey's end.

Mandy felt her eyes fill with tears as she pictured Ida and the cubs ahead of them, wading into the clear water of the lake to drink. They would gaze at every familiar oak tree and berry bush, every woodpile, cave and safe retreat.

Mount Ida, their range. The bears had faced the dark nights, the long walk, hunger, trucks, and guns to find it again. And now, in spite of everything, by some mysterious instinct, they were here.

Mandy murmured the best sounding word of all: 'Home!'

# Ten

A head peeped out above the long grass that grew by the shore of Cherokee Lake.

'Jill!' Mandy whispered. The cub's blunt black nose twitched, her ears were pricked. She looked this way and that.

'And Jack!' James saw a second head pop up. It was the cub with the collar whom they'd rescued from Dusty Owen's barn. He popped red berries into his mouth with his agile front paws.

Mandy sighed as the cubs fed on the berries and plants. Further off, knee deep in the rippling water, Ida stood and waited for fish. Mandy turned to Frank, who had just finished writing his notes for the study.

'Great piece of work,' he told them. 'We have a record of how many hours the bears spent travelling, when they stopped to eat and where they rested. We got a detailed picture of their behaviour all along the way. This is real important to our whole bear programme!' Frank took off his glasses and folded them into his top pocket. A smile split his face from ear to ear as he handed out chocolate.

Mandy savoured the sweet taste, enjoying the warm evening sun on her back as she watched the bears. 'What now?'

'Sleep!' James yawned.

'Yep. It's all over. I called your parents to give them the good news. They didn't want to wait for me to drive you up to Omaha Springs, so they said they'd come straight down to collect you.'

'Thanks.' She sighed happily. For the first time since they'd set eyes on Ida and the cubs, the bears seemed at ease. Jack and Jill had spotted some tall white birds with long, curved beaks standing at the water's edge. They gave chase. The ibis flapped their wings and rose noisily. Meanwhile, Ida waded deeper into the cool water, confident that the cubs were playing safely.

Then, in an instant, it all went wrong.

There was a blur, a dark shadow charging through the grass; it was a snarling beast with a massive head and snapping jaws.

Jill yelped and veered out of its path. She vanished in the long grass. But Jack wasn't quick enough. The charging animal had him in its sights. He backed into the water, fell and rolled.

'It's the bear we saw at the shut-in!' James came to his senses. 'He's attacking Jack!'

The bear cub yelped and sank under the water as the black bear pounced.

'He'll kill him!' Mandy cried. She leaped to her feet. *Wave your arms. Yell.* She remembered what to do as she ran to scare the attacker off.

But this time the bear didn't run. He'd moved in on this empty range after Ida and the cubs had been trucked out by the farmers. It was good territory; there was plenty of food and water, and lots of cover. He must have seen them at the shut-in and realised he would have a fight on his hands to keep it. Now here he was to protect his new home range.

Jack struggled beneath the strong, young bear, dodging his snapping teeth, powerless to escape from its grip – until Ida reached them.

Mandy had never seen anything like the anger of the mother bear. Ida surged through the water, mouth open, lips curled back. Then she reared on to her hind legs, towering over the intruder. A roar rose from deep in her chest. She swung through the air with her sharp claws, swiping him out of the way as she snatched Jack from his clutches.

The black bear howled. He tumbled sideways from the force of Ida's blow and fell into the water with a crash. Then Ida was at him again with her teeth and claws, going for his throat, savaging the intruder until he rolled over and submitted.

Ida stood over him, ready to plunge on top of him again. But the fight had gone out of the young bear. Ida was massive, a full grown female protecting her cubs. He knew the battle was lost. So he crept away, his coat streaming, head down, making for the shore.

Mandy watched him slink away. Ida saw him off, dropping on to all fours and harrying him up the hillside. The fight was over. Fierce Ida had made it plain whose territory this was.

James turned to check the cubs. He saw Jill creeping back through the grass, and Jack still cowering in the water. 'Mandy!' His voice came out high and breathless. 'Jack's been hurt! He's bleeding!'

Mandy jerked round to see the clear water stained red. The cub struggled to stand, then fell back. His head sank sideways and disappeared below a crimson surface.

They ran, all three of them, to drag Jack out of the water and carry his limp body on to the shore. Mandy dropped to her knees to take the cub's weight in her arms. she lifted him, while Frank cradled his head and James kept the other cub at bay.

Jill darted at them, nipping at their legs in a desperate effort to see them off, not knowing that they were trying to save her brother's life.

As they lay him on the ground, Ida hurtled back down the hill. The enemy had fled for good. Now she turned her attention to her cubs. She found Mandy and Frank crouching over Jack, who was bleeding from a deep gash across his nose. The mother bear nudged Frank away with her head, began to lick the cub's face as he whimpered and cried.

'It's OK,' Mandy soothed. She knew what to do when an animal was wounded. As long as Ida would trust her, Jack stood a chance. 'We'll help him!'

They needed to stop the flow of blood. The wound on his face was wide and deep. Mandy glanced round for some padding to press against the cut.

'Here!' James took off his T-shirt and handed it to her.

She screwed it up and pressed it hard against the gash. At first the blood welled up and soaked through, but she kept the pad firmly in place. 'It's slowing!' she muttered at last. 'Now we need to strap it with some kind of bandage.'

Ida kept on licking Jack, nudging him softly with her nose. She seemed willing to let Mandy work on. Jill crouched beside her, whimpering softly.

'Bandage?' Frank and James looked round helplessly. Then James went running for his rucksack, came back with another shirt which he tore into strips and handed to Mandy.

Swiftly she took the blood-soaked pad away and bound the clean bandage tight around the cub's muzzle. He was too weak and dazed to resist. Soon Mandy had the wound tightly strapped up.

'What now?' Frank got to his feet and stumbled against Ida. He rested one hand on her shoulder.

'We have to keep him covered. He's shivering from shock.' Mandy asked Frank for another spare shirt and laid it carefully over the cub's trembling body. She stroked his poor head, looking for other cuts made by the black bear's claws and teeth.

'Will he live?' The question tumbled out of James's mouth.

'I don't know,' Mandy replied. 'It depends how much blood he lost. He was already weak from the journey.' The cub's eyes were closing, his breathing was shallow. The signs weren't good. Her experience of helping her mum and dad at Animal Ark made Mandy realise that his chances were slim.

'He can't die now!' James said under his breath. 'Not after all he's been through. Do something, Mandy!'

'She's done all she can.' Frank put a hand on his arm. 'She's given him a chance.'

'. . . The wound should be stitched. We need the proper stuff: needles, antibiotics . . .' Mandy told Frank and James her worries. It was half an hour after the attack. They'd carried the cub out of the sun into the shade of a rock. Ida and Jill had retreated to a safe distance up the hillside and settled down to watch.

Mandy was still worried. She knew that the makeshift bandage wasn't good enough. Blood was still seeping through from the wound. 'Even if he gets over losing so much blood, he still might not make it.' There were infections he could pick up without the proper injections, he might be too weak to survive in the wild.

'Is he asleep, or unconscious?' James gazed down at Jack. The cub's eyes were closed, and they could just make out the shallow rise and fall of his ribs as he drew air into his lungs.

'A bit of both. He's probably drifting in and out of consciousness.' Mandy felt for his pulse; it was what she dreaded – weak and uneven.

Frank had wandered a short way off to think. 'I guess we could contact the nearest farm, get them to fetch a truck down here and drive the cub into the vet in Little Rock.'

'Let's do that,' James agreed. Anything was better than doing nothing.

'If Jack can survive the journey,' Mandy warned. Weak as he was, hanging on to life, the jolting drive into town might prove too much.

'Hey!' Frank strode back to join them. 'Do you believe in miracles?' He pointed along the lake shore to where a battered red truck came lurching across the rocks and pebbles. 'Isn't that the Owens' pick-up truck?'

Mandy jumped up to look. As the truck drew nearer, she recognised the old farmer's camouflage hat, his scrawny frame hunched over the wheel. And beside him someone was leaning out of the open passenger side window, waving and calling their names. 'Mum!' When Mandy saw who it was, she yelled at the top of her voice. 'Come quick. We need you!'

The truck crunched to a halt, the door flew open and Emily Hope came running. Then Mandy saw her father stand up in the back of the open-top truck and vault over the side. He carried a bag with him as he raced towards them.

'What now?' he yelled. 'What is it this time?'

Not one, but two vets had arrived to help save Jack's life!

'. . . Yep,' Mandy told Frank as she stood up to make room for her mum and dad beside the injured cub, 'I do believe in miracles.'

Adam Hope took syringes and needles out of

the first-aid kit in his rucksack and laid them out. Emily unstrapped the bloody bandage and examined the gash as Jack opened his dull eyes and blinked. She felt for his pulse, looked inside his mouth, then got to work on putting stitches into the wound. 'Touch and go,' she murmured as she worked.

They used antiseptic powder and injected the cub with an antibiotic. Then, having removed his collar, they gave him sugar solution through a tube down his throat.

'We don't want to move him,' Adam Hope decided, taking a quick look round. 'For one thing, the mother wouldn't like it if we took him away.' He'd spotted Ida and Jill waiting anxiously on the hill. 'For another, it's best to let him recover in his natural habitat.' He told James and Mandy to bring branches of brushwood to stack up against the rock as a kind of shelter.

So they fetched the wood and built a shield to hide Jack, while Mandy's mum and dad finished their work. Then they lined the hollow where the cub was lying with soft grass.

'His eyes are staying open now,' James whispered. 'That must mean he's getting better.'

Mandy knelt and peered inside the shelter they'd made. 'The wound looks nice and clean,' she said. She turned to Frank. 'It's getting dark. Do you think it's safe to leave him?'

'Sure.' He nodded towards Ida, who crept closer to see what had become of her cub. 'Here comes the best bodyguard in the world.'

'We'll come back tomorrow and see how he's getting on,' Adam Hope promised, putting his arm around Mandy's shoulder. 'He's comfortable and clean, and we've done all we can. For now, what he needs most is rest.'

'Me too,' Frank and James agreed in the same breath.

'OK, me too.' Reluctantly Mandy gave in. 'We've done all we can,' she repeated quietly to James as they sat in the back of Dusty's pick-up for the journey back to Omaha Springs. 'But is it enough?'

A REPORT ON THE HOMING INSTINCT OF THE BLACK BEARS OF LAKE CHEROKEE. Frank showed James and Mandy the cover of the study.

'I got it printed out on the office computer,' he told them proudly. It was three days after Ida and the cubs had returned home, and Frank had driven out to the lake specially to show them the report.

James opened the booklet. ' "Special thanks to James Hunter and Mandy Hope from Welford,

England. Without their help this study would not have been possible." ' He read out the words on the first page and blushed.

'It's true.' The scientist shook their hands and said goodbye. He was heading back from Little Rock to Omaha, to take up his study of Charlie Brown at Wolf Point. The Hopes and James were driving south, back to Florida.

'Will you write to us when we get back home?' Mandy asked him.

'Sure. I'll tell you how Charlie's getting along.' Frank watched them climb into the giant motor home which Adam Hope had driven down from Bear Creek. He prepared to wave them off from the shore of Cherokee Lake. 'You drive safely now!'

They had the map spread out on the dashboard, a tankful of fuel, a long day's drive ahead. But Mandy knew there was one more thing she wanted to do before they left. 'Please can we take one last look?' she asked.

Emily Hope smiled and nodded. 'You and James can go. We'll wait here.'

So the two of them ran along the shore, skirting the rippling water, leaping narrow streams that trickled down to the lake. It was early morning; Ida would be returning to her den after a night spent foraging in the hills.

There was the rock where they'd built Jack's shelter. The stack of brushwood was still in place these three days later.

'Slow down,' James whispered. 'We don't want to frighten him.'

So Mandy trod carefully as she came near to the den and peered inside. 'Empty,' she said under her breath, trying not to be scared. She stood upright and scanned the hillside. Where was Jack?

For a few minutes they waited. Rabbits bobbed through the grass, in and out of burrows. A grey squirrel scurried along the branch of a nearby tree. Then there was a heavier tread, the sound of leaves swishing and, twigs snapping.

'Here they come!' Mandy breathed.

Ida appeared out of the undergrowth, plodding home after her night in the open. She swayed as she walked, her belly full, her great head rolling from side to side. The sore on her foot had healed. There was no limp.

Then Jill came, quicker and noisier, using a leafy slope as a short-cut to slide down. She landed on the pebbled shore with a thump.

James grinned at Mandy. But she had her eyes fixed on the undergrowth. 'Come on!' she muttered. Until she saw with her own eyes, she wouldn't be happy.

*Chuff-chuff*! Ida turned impatiently to wait.

And Jack appeared from the bushes, head to one side, his pale, honey-coloured coat covered with leaves and twigs, ready to tumble down the slope after Jill.

But Ida wanted him close by her side. He was still weak from his injury. It was the first time he'd left the den and she refused to trust him with the rough play just yet. She coughed again to make him take the safe way down with her.

The cub obeyed, picking his way down to the lake. From where they stood, Mandy and James could see the nearly-healed wound on his face and sighed with relief.

They waited until all three bears reached the water. Ida turned and saw them, gazed for a few moments, then turned away to watch the cubs at play. Jill ran headlong, into the water, plunged deep, and swam out from the shore. Jack tested his way; he got one foot wet, then waited. The tiny waves sparkled. He watched them, tilted his head, then followed.

'. . . So, he's OK?' Adam Hope asked, as James and Mandy ran back and climbed into the cab of the motor home.

'He's been out all night by the look of him, and now he's swimming,' James reported. 'So he must be.'

Mandy stayed quiet. Her dad started the engine, and they rolled away.

Goodbye to her brave heroine and the two cubs. Mandy turned to look. Her last glimpse of Ida was of her dipping under the water, then standing knee-deep in the lake, shaking herself dry in a million golden droplets as the sun caught her in its early morning rays.

**If you like ANIMAL ARK –
you'll love JESS THE BORDER COLLIE!
A brand new trilogy from Lucy Daniels!**

**Here's an extract from Book 1, *The Arrival* . . .**

'Dad!' Jenny yelled across the farmyard.

Fraser Miles turned, and, at the sight of Jenny's worried expression, strode back across the yard towards her. 'What is it?' he asked urgently.

'I don't know,' Jenny replied anxiously. 'Nell seems distressed.'

Fraser followed Jenny into the stables where the sheepdog and her new-born puppies were lying. Nell was panting now, her flanks damp and hot.

Jenny watched as her father put a hand on Nell's side. 'There's another puppy on the way,' he said. 'But I was sure that there were only four. This one must be very small.'

'Is Nell going to be all right?' Jenny asked. 'She wasn't like this with the others. What's wrong, Dad?'

Fraser Miles's face was serious. 'She must be exhausted by now,' he explained.

Jenny closed her eyes and made a wish. *Please let them both be all right*. She didn't dare to watch. Nell looked up at her with mournful eyes as she struggled to give birth to this last puppy.

'There, girl,' Jenny whispered. 'Just a little longer. Be brave.'

The collie turned her head and licked Jenny's hand. Her body shuddered, then went still. Jenny felt the breath stop in her throat.

'It's OK now,' Fraser reassured her, scooping up a little bundle into his hands. 'It's over, old girl. Just you concentrate on your other four puppies.'

Her father's words rang in Jenny's ears.

'What do you mean, Dad? The last puppy isn't dead, is it?'

Fraser looked down at her and his usually stern expression softened. 'No,' he said gently. 'He isn't dead. But he might as well be. He'll never make a working dog.'

Jenny looked at the pathetic little bundle her father was holding. It was so tiny Fraser could easily hold it in one hand. He had torn away the birth sac from the puppy's head but there was no sign of the little animal breathing. Jenny touched a finger to the puppy's body. It was warm and she could feel his heart beating under his skin.

Then, as her father removed the rest of the sac,

the puppy breathed. 'It's going to live!' she cried.

'Look, Jenny,' her father said.

For the first time, Jenny noticed what her father had already seen. The puppy's right front leg was twisted at an impossible angle. 'His leg!' she cried. 'What happened to it?'

'It must have been growing like that for some time inside the womb,' Fraser Miles explained, cutting the umbilical cord and drying the puppy with a piece of old towel.

'Oh, the poor thing,' said Jenny, gently taking the puppy in her own hands. She laid him down beside his brothers and sisters. 'There,' she encouraged him. 'You feed too.'

But the puppy was far too weak. The bigger pups scrambled over him, pushing him out of the way. Even Nell pushed him away from her.

'What's wrong?' Jenny asked. 'Why is Nell rejecting him?'

'Instinct,' her father explained. 'She knows he won't survive. Look at him. He's so weak he can hardly breathe.'

'But he *is* breathing,' Jenny insisted. 'That must mean he wants to live.'

Fraser leaned over and laid his hand on the puppy's bad leg, testing it gently. 'I'd never be able to sell him,' he said.

'I'd look after him,' Jenny protested.

'You know the rules, Jenny,' Fraser Miles answered. 'Every animal on this farm has to earn its keep. This crippled little pup could never do that.'

Jenny blinked back tears. 'What are you going to do then?' she whispered.

Fraser looked at her in real concern. 'I'll have to put him down,' he said gently. 'It's the kindest thing for him. The other puppies will crowd him out. He won't get fed. He won't even get near his mother to keep warm. At least this way he won't be in pain. He won't suffer.'

Jenny swallowed hard. She knew what her father said was true. She had lived on a farm all her life. There was no room for unproductive animals on a farm.

The little puppy moved in her hands and yawned. The tip of a tiny pink tongue licked her finger. Jenny just couldn't let him go – not just yet.

'Can I have a little while to say goodbye?' she asked.

Fraser Miles bent over Nell. 'All right,' he said. 'I'll just wait with Nell to see she's OK after that last birth.'

'Thanks, Dad,' said Jenny. 'I'll take him into the

house. It's warmer there and Nell doesn't want him here.'

She was almost at the door when her father called her. 'Remember what I said, Jenny. Don't get too attached. That puppy has to go.'

Jenny nodded and looked down at the puppy. She knew what her father said made sense. But it was too late. It was *far* too late for common sense. She had already fallen in love with this puppy.

**If you'd like to read more – look out for *Jess the Border collie* in the shops from June!**

*Another Hodder Children's book*

## ANIMAL ARK FAVOURITES
### A short story collection

*Lucy Daniels*

*Mandy Hope loves animals more than anything else. She knows quite a lot about them too: both her parents are vets and Mandy helps out in their surgery, Animal Ark.*

Mandy and James catch up with old friends and make new ones along the way in this wonderful collection of nine Animal Ark short stories, featuring favourite animals and characters from the series in brand new adventures: Prince the pony riding to the rescue, Houdini the goat foiling a thief, Tess set for triumph in the sheepdog trials and Amber the kitten on the run once more . . .

## Order Form

## JESS THE BORDER COLLIE
*Lucy Daniels*

| | | | |
|---|---|---|---|
| 0 340 70438 1 | The Arrival | £3.99 | ❏ |
| 0 340 70439 X | The Challenge | £3.99 | ❏ |
| 0 340 70440 3 | The Runaway | £3.99 | ❏ |

*All Hodder Children's books are available at your local bookshop, or can be ordered direct from the publisher. Just tick the titles you would like and complete the details below. Prices and availability are subject to change without prior notice.*

Please enclose a cheque or postal order made payable to *Bookpoint Ltd*, and send to: Hodder Children's Books, 39 Milton Park, Abingdon, OXON OX14 4TD, UK.
Email Address: orders@bookpoint.co.uk

If you would prefer to pay by credit card, our call centre team would be delighted to take your order by telephone. Our direct line *01235 400414* (lines open 9.00 am–6.00 pm Monday to Saturday, 24 hour message answering service). Or you can send a fax on *01235 400454*.

| TITLE | | FIRST NAME | | SURNAME | |
|---|---|---|---|---|---|

| ADDRESS | |
|---|---|
| | |
| | |

| DAYTIME TEL: | | POST CODE | |
|---|---|---|---|

Alternatively please complete:
**Please debit my Visa/Access/Diner's Card/American Express (delete as applicable) card no:**

| | | | | | | | | | | | | | | | | |
|---|---|---|---|---|---|---|---|---|---|---|---|---|---|---|---|---|

Signature ..................................................... Expiry Date: ................................

If you would NOT like to receive further information on our products please tick the box. ❏

# ANIMAL ARK

*Lucy Daniels*

| | | | |
|---|---|---|---|
| 1 | KITTENS IN THE KITCHEN | £3.99 | ☐ |
| 2 | PONY IN THE PORCH | £3.99 | ☐ |
| 3 | PUPPIES IN THE PANTRY | £3.99 | ☐ |
| 4 | GOAT IN THE GARDEN | £3.99 | ☐ |
| 5 | HEDGEHOGS IN THE HALL | £3.99 | ☐ |
| 6 | BADGER IN THE BASEMENT | £3.99 | ☐ |
| 7 | CUB IN THE CUPBOARD | £3.99 | ☐ |
| 8 | PIGLET IN A PLAYPEN | £3.99 | ☐ |
| 9 | OWL IN THE OFFICE | £3.99 | ☐ |
| 10 | LAMB IN THE LAUNDRY | £3.99 | ☐ |
| 11 | BUNNIES IN THE BATHROOM | £3.99 | ☐ |
| 12 | DONKEY ON THE DOORSTEP | £3.99 | ☐ |
| 13 | HAMSTER IN A HAMPER | £3.99 | ☐ |
| 14 | GOOSE ON THE LOOSE | £3.99 | ☐ |
| 15 | CALF IN THE COTTAGE | £3.99 | ☐ |
| 16 | KOALA IN A CRISIS | £3.99 | ☐ |
| 17 | WOMBAT IN THE WILD | £3.99 | ☐ |
| 18 | ROO ON THE ROCK | £3.99 | ☐ |
| 19 | SQUIRRELS IN THE SCHOOL | £3.99 | ☐ |
| 20 | GUINEA-PIG IN THE GARAGE | £3.99 | ☐ |
| 21 | FAWN IN THE FOREST | £3.99 | ☐ |
| 22 | SHETLAND IN THE SHED | £3.99 | ☐ |
| 23 | SWAN IN THE SWIM | £3.99 | ☐ |
| 24 | LION BY THE LAKE | £3.99 | ☐ |
| 25 | ELEPHANTS IN THE EAST | £3.99 | ☐ |
| 26 | MONKEYS ON THE MOUNTAIN | £3.99 | ☐ |
| 27 | DOG AT THE DOOR | £3.99 | ☐ |
| 28 | FOALS IN THE FIELD | £3.99 | ☐ |
| 29 | SHEEP AT THE SHOW | £3.99 | ☐ |
| 30 | RACOONS ON THE ROOF | £3.99 | ☐ |
| 31 | DOLPHIN IN THE DEEP | £3.99 | ☐ |
| 32 | BEARS IN THE BARN | £3.99 | ☐ |
| | SHEEPDOG IN THE SNOW | £3.99 | ☐ |
| | KITTEN IN THE COLD | £3.99 | ☐ |
| | FOX IN THE FROST | £3.99 | ☐ |
| | SEAL ON THE SHORE | £3.99 | ☐ |

*All Hodder Children's books are available at your local bookshop, or can be ordered direct from the publisher. Just tick the titles you would like and complete the details below. Prices and availability are subject to change without prior notice.*

Please enclose a cheque or postal order made payable to *Bookpoint Ltd*, and send to: Hodder Children's Books, 39 Milton Park, Abingdon, OXON OX14 4TD, UK. Email Address: orders@bookpoint.co.uk

If you would prefer to pay by credit card, our call centre team would be delighted to take your order by telephone. Our direct line *01235 400414* (lines open 9.00 am–6.00 pm Monday to Saturday, 24 hour message answering service). Alternatively you can send a fax on *01235 400454*.

| TITLE | FIRST NAME | SURNAME |
|---|---|---|

| ADDRESS |
|---|
| |
| |
| DAYTIME TEL: | POST CODE |

If you would prefer to pay by credit card, please complete: Please debit my Visa/Access/Diner's Card/American Express (delete as applicable) card no:

| | | | | | | | | | | | | | | | | | |
|---|---|---|---|---|---|---|---|---|---|---|---|---|---|---|---|---|---|

Signature ..........................................................................

Expiry Date: ....................................................................

If you would NOT like to receive further information on our products please tick the box. ☐

# ANIMAL ACTION

If you like *Animal Ark* then you'll love the RSPCA's Animal Action Club! Anyone aged 13 or under can become a member for just £5.50 a year. Join up and you can look forward to six issues of Animal Action magazine - each one is bursting with animal news, competitions, features, posters and celebrity interviews. Plus we'll send you a fantastic joining pack too!

**To be really animal-friendly just complete the form - a photocopy is fine - and send it, with a cheque or postal order for £5.50**

Registered charity no 219099

**(made payable to the RSPCA), to Animal Action Club, RSPCA, Causeway, Horsham, West Sussex RH12 1HG. We'll then send you a joining pack and your first copy of** *Animal Action.*

# Don't delay, join today!

**Name** ..............................................................................................

**Address** ...........................................................................................

.................................................................................................................

.......................................................... **Postcode** ..............................

**Date of birth** ...................................................................................

**Youth membership of the Royal Society for the Prevention of Cruelty to Animals**

AACHOD2